HOT &

A HOSTILE OPERATIONS TEAM Novel

BOTHERED

LYNN RAYE

NEW YORK TIMES & USA TODAY BESTSELLING AUTHOR

HARRIS

www.**lynnrayeharris**.com

First Edition: August 2015
Library of Congress Cataloging-in-Publication Data

Harris, Lynn Raye
    Hot & Bothered / Lynn Raye Harris – 1st ed
        ISBN-13: 978-1-941002-07-0

1. Hot & Bothered—Fiction
2. Fiction—Romance
3. Fiction—Contemporary Romance

OTHER BOOKS IN
THE *HOSTILE OPERATIONS TEAM* SERIES

DEDICATION

To the Hotties.
Thanks for loving these books and asking for more.

PROLOGUE

EMILY ROYAL BIN YUSUF WAS JOGGING along the path in Rock Creek Park, listening to Fall Out Boy on her iPod and thinking about the paper she had due in her psychology class next week, when a man fell in beside her. It was broad daylight and there were plenty of people in the park, but the sudden appearance of a man at her side unnerved her.

After the life she'd led in recent years, she was still working on responding like a normal adult and not someone with a paranoia complex. But she wasn't there yet.

She told herself he was passing, that she was in his way, but he didn't pull ahead. And she stubbornly kept her gaze on the path, refusing to look at him though her heart was beginning to pound harder and her endurance was failing as a result.

Finally she slowed her pace and stopped as he kept going. Thank God.

She checked her Fitbit for her heart rate and started to walk. She hadn't gone as far as she wanted, but maybe it was time to head back to the apartment she shared with another student. That psych paper wasn't writing itself after all.

The man slowed up ahead. Then he turned and started jogging back toward her. He was tall and dark, intense and muscular like the Special Ops soldiers she knew. He was barely sweating as he approached. He passed her, then turned and fell in beside her again.

Emily thought about running off the path and screaming, but she told herself that was an overreaction. There were plenty of people here. Plenty of witnesses. Possibly he just wanted to hit on her. He was handsome enough, though he did nothing for her.

"How are you, Emily?"

She stumbled to a halt and whirled to face him. "How do you know who I am?"

"A lot of people know who you are."

Her heart thumped. "Did the colonel send you?"

Colonel Mendez was the leader of the Hostile Operations Team, a secretive black-ops group that had evacuated her from Qu'rim. Her sister worked for them. Victoria had done a lot to find her in Qu'rim, worked for some shady people, before she'd thrown her fate in with HOT. Emily didn't know details, but she knew Victoria had cut a deal with Mendez to give Emily a normal life again.

Or as normal as could be for the widow of a known terrorist leader. She'd been naïve when she'd gone to Qu'rim with Zaran, but she wasn't naïve any longer. Being married to Zaran would affect the rest of her life. It wasn't the same as a drunken binge or a drug arrest as a juvenile. This was bigger. She was on no-fly lists the world over. She could never hold a government job. Never have a security clearance.

And she couldn't, under any circumstances, confess her feelings to the one man who meant something to her. His career would be ruined if she did. Hell, he risked enough by talking to her, but she couldn't cut that thread. It terrified her to think of cutting it. So long as she had him in her life, even peripherally, she could survive what the world threw at her.

The stranger snorted. "Mendez didn't send me."

He lifted his head and let his gaze slide over the brown grass and bare trees in the park as if he were searching for something. Definitely a Spec Ops guy. And yet that didn't make her feel any better about him.

"Let's walk before we draw attention."

"I'm not going anywhere with you."

"Just walk with me, Emily. We'll stay on the path. I promise that you want to hear what I have to say."

She lifted her head. It was cold out, but she was warm from her jog—and from the adrenaline coursing through her. "And what could you possibly have to say that would interest me?"

"I'll tell you when we're walking."

She dragged in a breath as she considered him. Yes, she was scared—and she was intrigued too. Still, she was cautious. She'd learned to be. "Tell me who you are first."

The man grinned. "My name is Ian Black."

ONE

THERE WAS ONLY ONE WOMAN RYAN "Flash" Gordon wanted, and she was off-limits. Hugely off-limits. So off-limits that his balls tightened just thinking about the potential rage machine her sister would unleash on him if he touched her.

But that one woman had just walked into Buddy's Bar, where HOT hung out in their downtime, dressed in a pair of faded jeans and a leather jacket. Her blond hair was loose and flowing down her back, reaching nearly to her ass. The long strands curled at the ends, and Ryan imagined wrapping his fists in those locks and tugging her to him so he could ravage her mouth with his own.

She looked up from where she'd gone to stand with her sister, her gaze meeting his. Her brown eyes softened a little, and his heart kicked in his chest.

Goddamn, why had he let himself get tangled up in this? Why had he let her keep texting him, talking to him, calling him in the middle of the night so she could tell him about her day?

Emily Royal bin Yusuf—it was critically important to

1

LYNN RAYE HARRIS

remember the bin Yusuf part, because no one else was going to forget it anytime soon even though she'd dropped
her married name—was the saddest person he knew. And
no wonder, considering what she'd been through. He knew
she'd had drug and alcohol problems as a teenager, and he
knew that when she'd met Zaran bin Yusuf, the man had
given her what no one else could at that moment in her
life.

He'd given her understanding, and he'd given her
hope. Too bad the dude had decided radical Islam was the
path he needed to follow. He'd dragged Emily to Qu'rim,
and he'd terrorized her every bit as much as he'd terrorized nations. More, probably.

A hand clamped down on Ryan's shoulder. He
worked hard not to react, not to slam whoever it was into
the floor and ask questions later. Good thing, because Nick
"Brandy" Brandon was standing there grinning at him.

"Lighten up, Flash. Here's your beer." He handed
over the ice-cold bottle of Sam Adams.

"Thanks."

Brandy's expression grew serious as his gaze strayed
to his fiancée. Victoria Royal stood with Emily, their
heads bowed together as they talked. Victoria had quietly
set her beer aside the instant Emily appeared. Ryan knew
she wouldn't touch it again while Emily was at the bar.

"Victoria's worried about Emily," Brandy said.
"She's started dating some guy."

Ryan's stomach tightened. Yeah, he knew about that.
When Emily had asked him what she should do, he'd told
her to go with her gut. She hadn't replied for hours. Then
she'd told him she'd accepted the guy's invitation to see a
band at a bar.

2

It had been everything Ryan could do not to howl. He'd made sure, however, that she texted him her whereabouts. He'd been poised to leap into his car and go rescue her if necessary. Hell, he hadn't slept that night until he'd heard from her.

Then HOT had been on a mission and he'd been out of pocket for weeks. Weeks in which he'd gone crazy imagining Emily dating some guy, needing a friend to talk to and having nowhere to turn.

When Ryan had returned Stateside just a few days ago, he'd been relieved to find messages from her on his phone. He hadn't seen her until today though. And it was killing him that he couldn't wrap her up in a hug and tell her how glad he was to see her.

"I think Emily is stronger than anyone gives her credit for," he said, watching her again. And then he took a swig of his beer to cover the awkwardness as Brandy looked at him.

"Maybe she is," Brandy finally said before turning to watch Victoria and Emily. "God knows a lesser woman would have crumbled under the weight of everything that happened out there."

Ryan knew he meant Qu'rim and the mission that had almost ended in Brandy and Victoria dying. Until Emily saved them. She'd had to kill Zaran to do it, but she hadn't hesitated.

Ryan had killed before. It was the job, killing those who wanted to kill him. Protecting the nation. Stopping the bad stuff before it happened.

But Emily wasn't a black-ops soldier. She wasn't trained. She'd stabbed her husband with his own knife, and she was never going to forget the moment when the blade

3

sank into soft flesh and the man she'd once cared for bled out on the floor.

Ryan had met her for the first time only minutes after. She'd been covered in blood and mumbling "Oh God" over and over again. He'd tried to comfort her. Sometime in the next few days while her sister recovered from her own wounds, Ryan had found himself drawn to Emily's side.

She'd clung to him, figuratively, and she hadn't stopped in the months since that night. Nor did he want her to, even though he knew it would be best for her. Best for them both.

Victoria turned a worried glance toward Brandy, and he made for her side without another word. Ryan sat there, staring at the three of them and wishing like hell he had the right to go to Emily. Finally Brandy handed her a drink from the bar—a sugary Coca-Cola because Emily didn't do diet—and she slipped the straw between her lips.

A minute later she strolled away from Brandy and Victoria while their attention was on Matt "Richie Rich" Girard and his fiancée, Evie Baker, who'd just arrived. Evie was still brushing snowflakes from her jacket as Matt tugged her into his arms and wrapped her in a hug as he said something in her ear that made her laugh.

Domestic bliss.

Ryan envied them—envied all his teammates who'd found love—but he knew it was easier for some than for others. His gaze landed on Garrett "Iceman" Spencer and Grace Campbell. Now that was a pairing he'd have never expected, but somehow it worked. Grace softened Ice's edges. Ice roughened up Grace's polish. It was perfect.

"How are you, Ry?"

Ryan's entire body tightened at the sound of Emily's voice. She'd come up on him when he wasn't watching for her, and her presence socked him in the belly like always. He concentrated on keeping his breathing slow and even. "Same as when you asked me in your text last night."

Emily didn't get too close, but then she didn't stay away either. Her eyes were fixed on his face. Her cheeks were still pink from the cold weather, and she smelled like apples and cinnamon. He'd never pressed his lips to her skin, but he wanted to. Especially now, when he hadn't seen or heard from her in weeks.

"I missed you," she said softly.

He swallowed. "Nah, you just missed having someone you could bug with your econ homework."

She normally would have laughed at that. She didn't this time. She just shook her head. "No, it was you."

Ryan's fingers tightened on the beer bottle before he set it on the table behind him. "Guess I should go away more often if it makes you miss me."

He said it jokingly, which was his default setting for emotion. He'd learned early in life to never let anyone see how things hurt you. Always keep them guessing with a smile and a joke. It was the safest way.

"You'll always go away, Ry. And I'll always miss you when you do."

"You shouldn't say things like that. What will Caleb think?"

Her cheeks grew a touch pinker, and he instantly regretted his comment. "I broke up with Caleb."

He didn't like the way that made his heart leap. "Oh? Sorry."

She turned and leaned against the same table he was

leaning on. Her scent overwhelmed his senses, made him want to close his eyes and breathe in. It had been a hard slog out there in the desert, chasing after those assholes who'd taken a group of Americans hostage. The things they'd done to one of the Americans before HOT arrived… it was enough to make a hardened warrior want to cry.

"It's okay," she said.

"Did he…?" He didn't know what to ask. He only knew that if the guy had hurt her in any way, Ryan was going to go *Full Metal Jacket* on his ass in the next hour or so.

"He didn't do anything. But, well, I… I couldn't kiss him, Ryan. I tried, but I couldn't."

"It's only been a few months since…" They both knew since what. He cleared his throat. "It takes time. You don't get over that kind of thing overnight."

She turned to look at him. He could feel her eyes boring into his profile, but he refused to make eye contact.

"I *am* over it. I killed a man, but it's no different than what you and my sister do. Zaran was a terrorist. It was him or me—and I chose me."

This time he did look at her. At her small, waiflike form beside him. So delicate and pretty. She might have killed, but she wasn't a killer.

"I know that, Emily. You did what you had to do. I just don't think you should expect that life goes back to normal in a certain amount of time. It might take you another year to kiss a guy. Or maybe it'll be next week."

God, he hoped not. He didn't want her kissing anyone.

She snorted softly. "Who knows what the future will

bring?" She set her Coke on the table and stood. "Maybe I'll kiss someone tonight."

"Just don't do it in front of Victoria," he shot back. "She'll castrate the poor guy."

Emily shook her head. And then she straightened, looking fierce and unafraid. "She has to realize I can take care of myself. You all do, actually."

"Have I ever said you couldn't?"

"No. But you hover like a mother hen."

He felt the sting of that accusation. "I'm your friend. I'm supposed to care."

One pale eyebrow arched. "Yes, you're my friend. You'll always be my friend, won't you, Ryan?"

He didn't like her tone, the way she seemed a little hesitant. "Of course I will. We were in combat together. We'll be comrades forever."

She nodded. "Good. I'll hold you to that."

Then she drifted away, toward where Grace, Evie, Victoria, Olivia, Gina, Lucky, and Georgie were gathered together near a pool table. They weren't actually playing, but then neither was anyone else at the moment.

Evie appeared to be the center of that conversation. The women all smiled and hugged her. Clearly, this was a celebration of some kind.

Matt stood with the guys and Ryan got up to amble over. Whatever it was, he probably shouldn't miss it.

"Hey, Flash," Matt said, shaking his hand. The dude was smiling bigger than Ryan had ever seen him smile before.

"Richie. What did I miss?"

"Evie's pregnant."

"Wow, congrats," Ryan said. The rest of the guys

were grinning ear to ear. Jack "Hawk" Hunter, who'd been one of the quietest and deadliest dudes Ryan had ever known before he got married, looked positively amused.

"There goes the sleep," Hawk said. "For at least a few years anyway."

Matt rubbed a hand over his head, mussing his hair. "Yeah, I guess so. I'm still in shock." He turned to look at Evie, his expression softening into something Ryan never expected from these hardened guys. But every one of them who was in a relationship did the same thing.

"We're getting married right away. We'll have a formal ceremony at Reynier's Retreat after the baby comes. And I want you all to be there."

"Wouldn't miss it," Sam "Knight Rider" McKnight said, and everyone agreed.

Reynier's Retreat was Matt's family plantation in Louisiana. Ryan had seen pictures. The place was pretty spectacular. Like something out of *Gone with the Wind*.

Fresh beers arrived and everyone took one. Then Ryan lifted his and said, "To Matt and Evie and the littlest Girard."

There was a chorus of "Amen, brother," before they clinked bottles and drank.

They stayed at Buddy's for another hour, everyone laughing and joking, drinking beer—unless they were pregnant or had issues with alcohol—and generally having a good time letting off steam. Buddy's was a haven in many ways. Jack's wife, Gina, was a famous pop star, but when she walked into Buddy's, she was just another patron. That was the kind of thing that kept the guys coming back. Buddy's was home.

Emily didn't talk to him again. She was quiet, staying

on the periphery, until finally she went over and picked up her coat from the chair she'd draped it over. Victoria immediately went to her side, but Emily smiled and dropped her hair over the back of her jacket.

After a few words he couldn't hear, she hugged Victoria and walked toward the door. Before she stepped out, however, she turned and caught his gaze. Their eyes held for a long moment and his pulse thudded harder.

Then she stepped through the door and the moment was over.

TWO

SHE'D MADE HER CHOICE. Emily wiped a tear from her eye and kept on walking to her car, her back stiff and her chin up. She would do this thing, join Ian Black and his mercenaries for an important mission, and she would make a difference in this world. She spoke Arabic, particularly the Qu'rimi dialect, and she still knew people who had associated with Zaran.

She had a chance to put things right, to stop the Freedom Force from terrorizing innocent people, and she'd get her life back. No more government watch lists. No more no-fly. No more suspicions and mistrust.

Ian Black had promised. All she had to do was leave her life behind for the next few months and go to Acamar where a radical Freedom Force cell was gaining strength. He wanted her help to infiltrate and spy on the group. To do that, she'd need to use all her knowledge of their tactics and structure.

When it was over, she'd be free. But for now she had to leave everything behind and return to the desert. It wasn't the desert of Qu'rim, but it was close since Acamar shared a border with Qu'rim.

She just hoped Ryan and Victoria would understand. Those were the two people she cared about, the two she didn't want to disappoint.

Emily drove home and went into her bedroom where the empty carry-on suitcase she'd dragged out earlier lay. Her heart thumped. Tomorrow she was gone. In the morning she would walk out of this apartment and drive to Dulles where she'd meet Ian. Then it was a plane to Paris. She didn't know how he was going to get her onto a plane, even a private plane, since she still had to pass through TSA security checks, but he'd assured her it was possible.

Emily packed her summer gear. She'd left the abayas behind when she'd left Qu'rim, but she was going to have to start wearing them again. When she finished packing, she turned on CNN International and watched the news. She'd avoided it when she'd first returned. She hadn't wanted to see the videos of terrorists beheading innocent civilians, hadn't wanted to think that people like that existed, though she knew they did.

The Freedom Force didn't behead tourists. Yet. If they thought it would benefit them in some way, they certainly would. That much she knew.

Emily set the suitcase by the door and sank down on the bed to scrub her hands over her arms. She was chilled even though she wore a sweatshirt and jeans. She should get ready for bed, but there was no way she would sleep tonight.

She picked up her phone and clicked on her text messages. It hit her that Ryan was the one who usually left and went silent, but this time it would be her. And the thought of not seeing him again punched her in the throat and stole her breath.

Because it was possible she might not make it out alive. Possible this mission would go wrong and she'd be the one who didn't come home again.

She dropped the phone and pulled her hands over her face. She couldn't leave like this. Not without seeing him one more time. Not without touching him. It was selfish of her, she knew that, but it was also somehow necessary.

Emily grabbed her keys, picked up the suitcase, and hurried out the door. She drove into Maryland, her heart in her throat the entire way. What would she say when she got there? What would she do?

She didn't precisely know, but she knew she had to go to him.

When she pulled into the apartment complex where he lived, she sat with her hands on the wheel, staring at his apartment. He was on the ground floor. Number 112. She'd never been here before, but she knew.

Emily turned off the car and got out, locking it and then wiping her hands down her jeans. Her palms were moist even though it was winter. Her heart hammered as she walked into the narrow corridor between apartments. She stood at his door for a long minute, her breath frosting in the night air, before she summoned her courage and rapped on the metal.

She didn't hear any movement, but then the door whipped open and Ryan stood there in a pair of sweatpants and nothing else. His chest was bare, the hard muscles smooth and tanned and very, very defined. He was sweating, which told her he'd probably been working out. Tattoos ran down one arm, a mix of tribal decorations that she'd only ever partially seen before.

He didn't look surprised to see her, but then she knew he never would have opened the door without knowing precisely who stood on the other side.

Emily swallowed. She felt very small and very out of her element at that moment.

"What happened?" Ryan demanded. "Did that Caleb guy do something? Why didn't you text me?"

She shook her head and shivered. "No, nothing happened. I just… I had to see you."

She shrugged helplessly, and Ryan's eyes softened. He swore, but then he stepped back and motioned her inside. Not before his eyes skimmed the surroundings though.

Emily walked into his apartment, hugging herself tight. The furniture was sparse, but that didn't surprise her. She didn't know why, but after so many months of talking to him on the phone, texting him, she felt like she knew who he was.

And who he was wasn't very concerned about decor.

He crossed his arms and stood as far from her as he could get without leaving the room. Her courage faltered as his expression remained unchanged.

"You've never done this before, Emily. What's going on?"

She sank onto the edge of his couch, deflated a little now that she was here. "I missed you, Ry. I told you that. And seeing you at the bar, not being able to touch you if I wanted to… it kills me."

She'd never said anything like that to him before, and his expression was a mix of shock and regret. Did he want to be able to touch her too? God, she hoped so.

"Emily." He shoved a hand through his hair. The ends

stood up because his hair was damp. On someone else it would have looked ridiculous. On him it was sexy as hell. Everything about him was sexy.

Which scared her, because she hadn't been with a man in a very long time. Zaran had lost interest at a certain point. No, not precisely lost interest. He'd had to keep himself clean and pure, he'd said. And since she wasn't able to give him a child, there had been no point in continuing to sully himself.

Sully himself. As if she were a pool of mud or blood or some other unspeakable substance.

She bowed her head to get hold of herself again. Ryan was there, kneeling on the floor beside her, his hand going beneath her chin and forcing her to look at him.

He had pale blue eyes that reminded her of a wolf sometimes, but not now. Not when they were soft and worried like this.

His mouth was the sexiest thing she'd ever seen, his lips full and kissable, the top lip slightly less full than the bottom. And there was a dip in that lip, a sexy little dip where she could put her tongue if he were hers.

How many lucky women had kissed Ryan Gordon and sucked on that lip before? Oh, she didn't want to know. Hot jealousy speared her at the thought.

"You can tell me," he said. "Whatever it is, you can tell me. Haven't I been a good friend?"

She nodded. And then she reached out and wrapped her fingers around his wrist. His eyes darkened for a second, or maybe she'd imagined it. But there was a fire in her fingertips, a fire that raced through her body and lit up nerve endings she'd thought were dead.

"I want you to kiss me, Ry. Please kiss me."

He didn't pull away, but this time the look in his eyes was panic. She didn't mistake that for one second. His grip on her chin tightened a little.

"Emily, don't ask that of me. Please don't ask it."

She dragged in a breath. "Am I that unattractive? That repulsive?"

She feared she was, even if it was an irrational fear. The mirror told another tale, but maybe there was something else. Something she couldn't fix no matter how hard she tried.

"Repulsive? God, no. You're the most beautiful woman I know. How could you think that for even a second?"

She laughed without humor. "Forgive me for having a hard time with this, but I asked you to kiss me and you acted like I wanted you to eat a worm or something."

He cupped her face in both his hands, his broad palms warm against her cheeks. She couldn't help but sigh. And shiver, because need was a strong drumbeat in her core right now. She didn't know if she could let him do more than kiss her, but she wanted him to.

"I can think of nothing I'd rather do than kiss you," he said fiercely. "But it would change everything if I did."

"Maybe I want it to change." She closed her eyes. "Wait, no. I know better. I know we could never date like normal people. I wouldn't want you to lose your job because of me. And you would, I know that. I'm *persona non grata*. Just hanging out with you guys like I did tonight is bad, but Colonel Mendez makes that much possible. I don't know how, but I know he does. If it weren't for him, I'd have never seen any of you again after Qu'rim."

Ryan swallowed. "The colonel is a powerful man.

More powerful than some generals I can think of, which is good for us. But he can only do so much."

"I know. I'm grateful for the life I have… but I want more." She hesitated for a long moment. And then she blurted out the truth. "Just once, I want you. I missed you so much."

He leaned forward until his forehead touched hers. They were still, silent. She smelled the warmth of his skin, felt the soft exhalations of his breath, and her heart ached.

"I've wanted to touch you like this for a very long time. Just touch you."

The ball of emotion in her chest hurt. "Then touch me. Touch me the way you want. If I'm ever going to be with anyone again…" She gulped. "I don't know that I can, quite honestly. But if there's a chance, it's with you."

Zaran hadn't raped her, but he'd taken delight in physically punishing her the deeper he sank into his mania. She'd trusted him once, and he'd betrayed that trust. He'd turned into someone completely different from the kind, sweet young Muslim man he'd been when they'd met in New Orleans. It still filled her with anguish to think about the man he used to be.

She'd killed Zaran in self-defense—but he'd killed the Zaran she'd fallen for long before that day. She'd been a widow for years before she'd become a widow in truth.

Ryan sucked in a breath. And then he let her go abruptly and stood. Her heart sank.

"I'm going to shower and change." He picked up a remote and handed it to her. "Watch something if you like. We'll talk when I'm done, okay?"

She took the remote, but she didn't turn on the television. Instead, she watched him walk into his room and shut the door. She thought about leaving. She couldn't do it. This was the last time she'd see him, maybe forever, and she wasn't walking out of here without at least one kiss.

Emily finally turned on the television and flipped to the news. A reporter talked about the growing radicalism of the Islamic splinter groups in the Middle East. Her heart skipped and her pulse throbbed as a video of a Qu'rimi militant with a balaclava on his head and an assault rifle in his hand gesticulated to a video camera.

Death to the American infidels. Death to Western capitalism. We will find you and we will crush you. You are not safe. We will not rest until we have killed every American on this earth. We will not rest.

It was the same rhetoric as always, but it chilled her nonetheless. She'd heard it preached in the camps, and she'd heard them plan assaults against civilian targets as a means of inspiring terror and change.

But that kind of assault didn't lead to change. It led to war and death.

Emily turned off the television and fell back against the cushions. The reality of what was about to happen to her life hit her. She'd agreed to go back, to be a part of that world again. The madness and fear she'd despised would be part of her daily existence once more.

She put her hands over her face and sat there, breathing deeply and praying that when morning came, she would still have the strength to join Ian Black.

She could back out. She knew that. She could simply go back home, unpack, and go about her life.

But it was half a life, wasn't it? No matter how hard she worked or how good she was, the damage she'd done when she'd married Zaran would be with her for the rest of her days. No man would ever want her when they under-stood she couldn't even go on a fucking cruise to the Car-ibbean, much less fly to Paris for the trip of a lifetime. How did you explain those things to a potential partner?

No, she wasn't backing out. She wasn't giving up this chance to make things right again. It was one mission. One critical mission. She could do this, and then she'd be back home and maybe everything would be better than ever.

She heard the shower turn on. She pictured the spray, pictured Ryan standing beneath it, his body tanned and hard. She pictured herself there, imagined running her hands over his muscles, imagined him kissing her, sliding inside her, taking her to heaven.

Emily stood and walked toward the bedroom.

THREE

RYAN STOOD UNDER THE SPRAY and let the water pummel him. He'd been doing push-ups when Emily knocked on his door. He hadn't expected anyone, but when he'd looked out the peephole and seen her standing there, his heart had dropped to his toes.

He'd thought something was wrong with her. He'd been ready to slay dragons for her. Except he couldn't slay the one dragon she asked him to kill. Touching her, kissing her—it was wrong. She'd had a rough life with a maniac, and she didn't need to be a part of the kind of life Ryan led.

She needed a man who could be there for her, not a man who dropped everything and disappeared for weeks on end. A man who might not return. Danger was a regular part of his life, and Emily didn't deserve that. She'd had enough adversity to last her a lifetime.

Then why do you keep talking to her, asshole?

Yeah, why did he? That was the one thing he couldn't seem to stop doing even though he knew he should. Every time he said to himself that this was it, this was the day he

19

told her he couldn't keep texting with her and talking to her, he couldn't make himself say it. The thought of not hearing her voice made a ball of ice form in his gut. So he let himself have a pass that day. And the next and the next.

Now it had come to this. She was here, telling him she wanted him, and he still couldn't make her leave.

Ryan turned his face up and let the water flood down over his eyes and nose for a long minute. Then he stepped back and took a deep breath, slicking his hand over his head as he did so.

He turned off the tap and grabbed a towel, wrapping it around his waist and stepping from the shower. He'd needed these few minutes away from her so he could shore up his defenses. But what if she hadn't waited? What if he walked out into the living room and it was unoccupied?

Maybe that would be best. Yet it also made him feel hollow inside. And cowardly, because he shouldn't need her to make the decision he was supposed to make.

Ryan stalked into his bedroom—and ground to a halt at the sight of Emily sitting on his bed. Her golden hair gleamed in the light of the lamp, framing her face in a halo. She looked like an angel sitting there, so sweet and achingly lovely—and clothed, thank God, because he hated to think what would have happened to him if she hadn't been.

She shrugged and gave him a shy smile. "I wasn't brave enough to be naked when you cmerged. But pretend I am, okay?"

Leave it to Emily to go right to the heart of the matter. "I'm not sure that's a good idea."

"Do you want me, Ryan?"

His cock was going to do the answering for him in about thirty seconds. His blood was rushing south, and things were in motion no matter how hard he tried not to let it happen.

"You're a beautiful woman. I'm a man who likes women. I think you know the answer."

Her fingers went to the buttons of her shirt, and his heart skipped several beats.

"I know you think I'm fragile. And maybe I am, but I know if I can ever do this again, ever be whole and enjoy sex, it has to be with you. Tonight."

He didn't deny the fragile part, though it was in direct counterpoint to what he'd told Brandy earlier. Yeah, he thought she was fragile. And stronger than hell. She was an enigma to him.

"Jesus, Emily. You couldn't kiss the guy. So what? That doesn't mean you need to come over here and have sex with me just to prove you can."

Her fingers were still moving down the buttons, still slipping them free, until he could see a hint of lace and a line of skin from her collarbone to her waist.

She got to her feet and pulled the shirt from her jeans. Then she let it fall down her arms. Her breasts were full for a small girl, and her skin was so pale and creamy. He might have made a noise of frustration at the sight of all that skin.

His cock was definitely interested now. No more hiding what was happening south of the border.

Her gaze slipped down to the tent in his towel. She swallowed, and he was engulfed with a wave of tenderness for her.

"Emily…" When she looked up at him, he smiled softly. God, she was killing him. "Is this really what you want?"

"Yes. You, Ryan. Just this once if that's all it can be. I promise I won't come over here again. I won't ask you for more. I won't act like this is something it's not."

"You have to understand…" He blew out a frustrated breath. "You've been through a lot these past few years. I don't want to hurt you. I don't want to be another black mark in your life."

She took a step toward him and then another. He didn't move as she stopped in front of him and put a hand on his arm. She ran her fingertips lightly up his forearm, his bicep, across his chest. What she said next pierced his heart.

"You aren't a black mark. You're the brightest spot there is."

Emily's heart was about to pound out of her chest. But she was running out of time, and if this night slipped away and she didn't kiss this man—make love to him— she might never have another chance.

No, she would *never* have another chance. Because even if she survived working for Ian Black, Ryan wouldn't ever want her again. She was about to betray him—betray them all—in a big way. Not because she was doing any- thing wrong, but because they wouldn't want her to do it. Colonel Mendez had never offered her this chance. She was certain that had everything to do with Victoria. And maybe Ryan too.

They were too protective, too worried. She loved them for it, but she also felt more and more suffocated as the days went by.

Her fingers glided over his skin, skimmed the planes of muscle. He stood very still and let her touch him, but he couldn't hide the reaction beneath his towel. Swarms of butterflies swirled in her belly as she reached for the edge of his towel and unhooked it.

It fell to the floor, revealing hot, hard muscle and a very stiff cock.

"Oh," she breathed.

He caught her hand before she could reach for him, and her gaze collided with his. He looked like a lion ready to pounce. A lion currently working very hard not to do so.

"I should tell you to get the hell out of here… but I can't. God help me, I can't."

"That's good," she whispered. "Because I think I will die if you send me away."

He dragged in a harsh breath. "If at any moment you're scared, you need to tell me. Don't stay quiet and hope it gets better."

She put her hand on his stubbled cheek. "How could I be afraid of you? You took care of me in Qu'rim, and you've been a friend to me through everything. I'm not afraid, Ry."

Yes, she'd wondered if she could be intimate with a man again, but she didn't wonder anymore. She knew, because the moment his body was revealed to her, wetness and longing had flooded all the darkest recesses of her inner core.

Nothing Ryan could do would scare her. He was too good to her, always had been, and she didn't fear him. He

23

was the only man—the *only* man—who could touch her this way.

He turned his head and pressed a kiss into her palm, and she shuddered with the hot sensation flowing through her nerve endings. Her clit swelled and tingled, her folds grew wetter, and her pussy ached in a way she'd almost forgotten. She hadn't felt desire in so very long.

Ryan hooked her arm around his neck and tugged her in, flush to his body. Their skin met, his hot and damp from his shower, hers hot from looking at him.

He slid a broad hand down her back, over her ass, and flexed his hips against her. He was big and hard and far stronger than she was—but she didn't fear. He wouldn't hurt her. Never.

His skin against hers was heaven. She pressed her mouth to his chest, dragged her tongue across the taut muscle until she found his nipple. He stiffened and swore when she sucked it into her mouth.

And then the world tilted and she realized he'd swept her up into his arms. He carried her over to his bed and laid her down on it. While she watched the play of dark and light across his beautiful body, he unzipped her jeans and tugged them down her body. Her panties and bra followed in short order.

Then he was sitting back on his haunches and staring at her. His cock leapt, the only part of him that didn't seem to obey the command to stay still.

"You're beautiful, Emily. Everything I imagined and more."

She felt a little shy lying in his bed, which was silly. "You imagined this?"

He snorted. "Pretty much every day since I met you."

That thought made her stomach flutter. He'd been thinking about her, and she hadn't known. She'd spent so many nights wondering if he was even the tiniest bit attracted to her or if he thought of her like a little sister. Because the longer she'd known him, the more she'd wanted him.

He'd been off-limits though. Still would be if she weren't leaving tomorrow morning.

"I imagined it too."

He stretched out over top of her, his body so close but not quite touching hers as he held himself up with his powerful arms.

"So many things I want to do to you, Emily."

She put her arms around his neck and tugged him down. "Then do them. Please, please do them. But start with a kiss, because that's what I want most right this minute."

Her eyes closed as his head descended. His lips touched hers. It was a featherlight touch, a tease really. No tongue. Just lips, soft and perfect. That bow in his upper lip—oh, that bow. She darted her tongue out and touched it, and he shuddered.

Then his mouth captured hers in a hot, thrilling kiss that curled her toes and sent syrupy heat pumping through her veins. She opened beneath him, moaning when his tongue touched hers. Their mouths fit perfectly, and their tongues slid and dueled and tasted for what seemed like hours.

He kissed her for a long while, gently sometimes, harder other times. Her nipples were tight little points that scraped against his chest, begging for his attention, but he wouldn't leave her mouth, wouldn't stop tasting her lips.

It was the most intimate experience she'd ever had. She hadn't had many lovers, but the ones she'd had were always eager to get to the main course.

Not Ryan. He kissed her like that was his sole purpose in life, though she could feel the hard swelling of his cock against her pubic bone.

And suddenly she didn't care about anything but having him inside her. She didn't need another second of foreplay. She just needed his mouth on hers and his cock deep inside.

Emily shifted her body, opening her legs and wrapping them around him. He groaned as he slid one hand down her side, shaping her, learning her texture, cupping her ass and lifting her against him.

"Please, Ryan," she begged, tilting her hips, seeking his hard cock. "Please."

He didn't refuse her. He shifted, and then she felt the blunt head of his penis as he entered her body. She gasped as he filled her, moaned when they were fully joined skin to skin.

"Are you okay?" he asked, his eyes searching hers.

"Yes. Kiss me again. I need you to kiss me."

His mouth took hers once more. It felt too good, almost too wonderful to bear. Emily locked her ankles around his waist as he began to move. He was slow at first, controlled. And then he tore his mouth from hers as the tension spiraled higher and he buried his face against her neck, his body pumping into hers faster and harder than before.

Emily caught him close. She flung her head back, surprised at the fresh heat flaring to life in her core. She'd never come like this, never with a man inside her, but as

Ryan moved against her, she knew it was going to happen. Joy filled her as she arched into him and thrust her hips up to meet him.

The pressure built and built until it caught her by surprise and flung her out over the edge. She held on for long seconds—and then she let go, falling into pleasure so intense it stole her breath away.

Ryan jerked backward, and then he was spilling onto her belly, his warm semen jetting onto her damp skin as he wrapped his hand around his cock and finished that way.

He got up and grabbed the towel he'd been wearing, cleaning her where he'd spilled himself onto her body. She didn't know what to say, how to express what he'd given her tonight.

"You didn't have to do that," she told him softly. "Pull out, I mean."

He looked fierce. "Yeah, I did. I should have protected you better than this—"

"I can't get pregnant." Tears filled her eyes as she said it. She'd never voiced it to anyone before now, and it hurt to say. Surprisingly, since she'd never been certain if she wanted kids anyway.

Ryan's eyes filled with sympathy—and maybe even relief. She didn't like to think of him being relieved they wouldn't have a baby together, but it was the reality of her life.

"Sweetheart, I'm sorry."

She sucked in a breath. His sympathy had the power to break her if she let it. "No, it's okay. You're relieved, and I get it. We got a little carried away... I should have told you it was okay before."

He shook his head. "You still deserved better. You

don't know who I've been with or what I might have caught."

She couldn't help but laugh just a little. "Ryan, you work for a highly specialized military outfit that wants to know if you so much as sneeze. I'm pretty sure you're okay."

He finished wiping her clean and threw the towel on the floor. "Yeah, guess that's true."

She felt a little shy as his gaze slid over her. She sat up and tugged her knees up, wrapping her arms around them. "Thank you," she said. "That was amazing."

She couldn't read his expression at all. He reached out and skimmed his fingers over her arm.

"Any regrets?"

A million of them, but none that involved him. "No," she whispered, dropping her gaze.

He tilted her chin up and searched her eyes. "Thank you for trusting me. I know it can't be easy for you."

She smiled. It was easy because it was him. "You've always been so good to me. I appreciate it more than you know."

He turned and sat back against the headboard, then pulled her into his arms. "You deserve happiness, Emily. You deserve everything good in life. And you deserve to be treated like the special woman you are."

She wrapped her arms around his as they sat there together. There was so much she wanted to say to him. So much she couldn't say. Somehow, Ryan had become her best friend. But how did you tell your best friend you were about to do something he definitely wouldn't want you to do?

"I wish we'd met under different circumstances," she

said quietly. "I wish so much was different."

He hugged her tight. Then he nuzzled her hair aside and spoke in her ear. "The only thing I wish is for you to be happy and safe."

She turned in his arms, tilted her face up to his. "I am happy when I'm with you."

He looked torn, intense, and she knew he was thinking they couldn't do this again. But he didn't know the real reason—and she wasn't going to share it with him.

"Kiss me, Ryan," she whispered.

His head dropped to hers. Everything faded but the heat between them.

FOUR

Two months later…

"FLASH, READY ROOM. NOW."

Chase "Fiddler" Daniels had just peeked his head around the corner of the team storage room and barked out the words before disappearing again. Ryan stood and opened his locker, stowing the gear he'd been checking for worn areas, before heading down the corridor and into the ready room.

When he walked inside, his teammates were all there. So was Echo Squad, another team they often worked closely with on assignments. Cade Rodgers, Echo's leader, nodded at him as he went over and sat next to Fiddler. Cade was a big motherfucker, tall and broad and about as mean as a rattlesnake. Just the kind of guy you wanted in your corner.

Then again, all the men in this room—and the two women, of course—were the kind you'd want in your corner.

Fiddler gave Ryan a look. It was one of concern and

puzzlement. Hell, all the guys had been looking at him like that for the past two months. They knew something was wrong. They just didn't know what.

But it had been going on since they'd learned Emily had left the country with Ian Black. Fucking Ian Black. Ryan's gut clenched tight. If he ever got in a room with that bastard again, he'd kill him. Didn't matter if the dude was on their side—or at least he'd appeared to be at last count—Ryan was going to kill him for involving Emily in whatever scheme he had going.

Ryan clenched his fists. It didn't matter how many days had passed since that last night with her, he still couldn't fathom that she'd walked away from her life— from him—the way she had. She hadn't told him a fucking thing! She'd lied to him that night. Lied about everything.

She'd made love to him for hours and then left him to return to the Middle East. The last time she'd gone to the desert with a man, the experience had chewed her up and spit her out and changed everything for her.

Jesus. Ryan scrubbed a hand over his face.

He still didn't understand. He *refused* to understand.

He looked at Victoria, at the tight lines around her mouth, and he knew she didn't understand either. She'd been filled with rage the day Mendez delivered the message from Black. Victoria had wanted to hop on a plane and go to the desert right away. Ryan had wanted to go with her, and to hell with everything else.

But Colonel Mendez had rightly pointed out that they had about as much chance of walking into any part of Qu'rim or the surrounding states and extracting her safely as a snowball had of surviving a furnace. They didn't even know if she was actually there. She could be anywhere, and until they knew more, they couldn't do a fucking thing about it.

Every day since then, Ryan had grown angrier and angrier. He felt... betrayed. Used. Cheated on, and that was a ridiculous notion considering they'd only ever been together once.

But they'd been friends for months, and he'd thought Emily could tell him anything.

Anything but the fact she was doing something crazy like leaving the country with Ian Black. What if she was fucking Black now? Ryan couldn't even see straight when he thought like that.

Colonel Mendez walked in, and everyone in the room shot to attention. He looked them over for a long minute before he spoke.

"At ease."

They sat down again as he went over to the computer console and tapped on some keys. A map of Acamar appeared on the whiteboard hanging on one wall.

"We've just gotten notice that a group of archaeologists working in the Kuma Desert have been taken hostage by a Freedom Force cell. One of the archaeologists is pregnant."

"Shit," someone said.

That sentiment was echoed by everyone in the room.

Mendez stood with hands on hips, looking every bit as angry as a lion with a thorn in his paw.

"We've been tasked with the rescue." His gaze slid over them, hard, angry, and Ryan knew that something else was coming. Something that none of them was going to like. "Our contact on this mission is an old friend to HOT."

Ryan's gut churned at the twist on the word *friend*. He didn't like where this was going. He knew, deep down, the name that Mendez was about to say—and it filled him with a kind of helpless rage he'd never felt before.

"Ian Black," Mendez continued, "has an asset inside the Freedom Force cell. He's getting his information from this asset and passing it through channels. We don't know where the archaeologists are being held, but once we get boots on the ground in Acamar, we'll work with Black and his team to locate and extract them."

"Can we trust Black's information, sir?" Fiddler asked.

It was probably the politest thing anyone could say. Ryan couldn't form a coherent sentence, much less ask something so nice as whether or not Black could be trusted. As far as he was concerned, Black could *never* be trusted.

But he'd gladly take the opportunity to work with the man on this mission. Because once he got Ian Black in his sights, he wouldn't rest until he knew precisely where Emily was.

He glanced at Victoria. Her mouth had flattened, and Brandy had moved closer to her. Yeah, she was pissed as hell at her former boss—and she'd been one of the few people who'd ever defended him.

Ryan didn't think she'd defend him now.

"Victoria, you're sitting this one out," Mendez said coolly.

It wasn't unexpected considering the circumstances, but Victoria looked surprised nonetheless.

"Sir, I can do the job."

"I know you can, but I think it's best if you don't.

You're emotionally compromised. Your sister went to join Black, and I don't need to worry about the inevitable explosion when you two meet up again. The hostages are our priority, not a family feud."

"Yes, sir," Victoria said, her voice as tightly controlled as a spring. The fury in her words was unmistakable to anyone who knew her, though. "Does this mean Emily is in Acamar, sir?"

"Yes. I am assured she's safe."

"And will you bring her home?"

Mendez's gaze didn't falter. "If that's what she wants, yes."

Victoria swallowed and nodded, and Mendez let his gaze slide across everyone there.

Ryan's pulse thumped as he waited for the colonel to single him out next. But that would mean Mendez somehow knew about Ryan's relationship with Emily—and he was pretty certain no one knew. He'd been careful. She'd been careful.

Or so he'd always thought.

Mendez turned back to the screen and called up another slide. Ryan breathed a sigh of relief as the colonel moved on with the planning. He informed them they'd be on a plane tonight and on their way to the zone. They would arrive in the city of Al-Izir and make contact with Ian Black and his mercenaries. Hopefully by then Black would have information about the hostages' location. If not, HOT was going to bunk in the compound with Black's mercenaries and wait for the coordinates.

Ryan didn't like that option. A quick glance around the room told him that no one else did either. Especially Iceman, who'd fought with Black when it appeared the man was responsible for trying to kidnap Grace Campbell.

After an evening involving a dunk in the Tidal Basin and a jail stay for both Ice and Black, they'd learned the mercenary was actually on their side. He'd been embedded with the group seeking to kidnap Grace Campbell, but he'd been working with Mendez when it came time to rescue Grace.

That didn't mean a damn thing to Ryan. So Black had been on their side *that time*. There was no guarantee he would be this time. His loyalties were unpredictable at best and traitorous at worst. He didn't care about people. If he did, he never would have recruited Emily.

That's what killed Ryan every day. Not knowing if she was okay or scared out of her mind. Wondering where she was. Who she was with. Wondering if Black was touching her the way Ryan had touched her.

He dipped his chin to his chest and studied the floor beneath his boots. Anger rushed through him, filled him so full he felt like he would burst at the seams with a single touch to his body. It was too much like when he was a kid and he'd been angry and hurt because his mother had left. He'd been fucking helpless to fix a damn thing, and he'd hated it.

He'd given her so many chances, kept expecting her to turn up at his games or for the weekends he was supposed to spend with her, but she didn't. Or if she did, she was high or drunk or just manic. Self-medicating when she should have taken the meds the doctors gave her instead.

He could still see his dad's sad face. Still hear his dad's voice. "She's not coming today, buddy. She's not feeling too well."

That had been code for she was too fucked up, but he

hadn't known it at the time. His dad, God bless him, had never said a bad word about his mother. It had taken getting older and losing the rose-colored glasses he'd viewed her with to make him realize the truth.

Maybe he'd had rose-colored glasses with Emily too. Maybe her vulnerability and sadness had masked the truth from his eyes.

His belly tightened at the thought even as his heart rebelled.

Just like when he'd been a confused kid wanting his mother to care about him.

Not the same thing. Not the same.

But it felt remarkably the same deep inside, goddammit.

"I know you don't like this," Mendez said after he'd finished with the logistics. "I know you don't want to sit in Al-Izir with Ian Black, but time is of the essence with this one. We have to be ready to act the minute we know the location of the hostages."

The faces around the room were stony, determined. And then they all spoke as one.

"Sir, yes, sir!"

Mendez nodded and looked at his watch. "Six hours until go. You know the drill."

FIVE

THE KUMA DESERT WAS A WASTELAND, and Al-Izir was right in the middle of it. The sand stirred up in whirlpools as something too dry and hot to be called a breeze scoured the desert floor.

Emily wanted to stop and pull down her abaya so she could take a drink from her waterskin, but she had to keep going. It wasn't that far to Ian Black's compound. She just had to tough it out. Lately, no matter how hydrated she was, how rested, the second she got out into the heat, she wilted. The heat of Acamar was taking it out of her, which was surprising considering how long she'd dwelt in Qu'rim's climate. They were the same, for heaven's sake.

The scents of burning meat wafted on the air, and her stomach rebelled. She put her hand to her mouth and hurried past the street vendor. When she reached a door on a side street, she took out her key and slipped it into the lock. It looked like a simple key lock, but she knew it was actually wired to a security system. Someone could steal her key, and they could use it to enter, but they wouldn't get very far with the cameras trained on the entry. She looked up into the camera, making sure it captured her face, before she passed into a shaded inner courtyard and leaned back against the wall. She searched beneath her abaya for the tube of her waterskin, sucking on it gratefully when she located it.

The water was warm, but still welcome.

"You okay, Emily?"

She looked up to find Rascal staring down at her. Rascal was a big man, bald, and about as gentle as a kitten. Or at least he was with people he liked. She suspected he was quite scary when he didn't like someone. He was, like many of the men here, a former soldier of some sort. She just wasn't sure for whom. Sometimes he had the trace of a foreign accent, but just when she thought she had a handle on it, it disappeared again and she was left wondering if she'd imagined it.

"Yes, fine, thanks."

He shook his head. "You look green."

She felt green, but she wasn't going to say it. "Not used to the heat, I guess."

He snorted. "You used to live out here."

"Been away too long."

He sniffed. "Looks like we've got company coming. Boss man says we're working with someone on this thing with the archaeologists."

Her stomach twisted. "Did he say who?"

"Nope." Rascal picked up the case he'd been carrying —guns, most likely—and slung it over his shoulder. "Got to get this stuff sorted. You go on inside and get some cold water, Em. Lie down a while and you'll feel better."

"Thanks."

Rascal tipped his head and kept on going. Emily

made her way deeper into the inner courtyard and entered the main dwelling. She'd quickly learned once she got out here that Ian Black had quite the network of spies, soldiers, and equipment. He was set up as well as anything she'd seen when the Hostile Operations Team had rescued her last year. Except his guys were a little on the rawer side. A little less polished and a lot more... mercenary.

Or maybe that was just her imagination. But they weren't quite like the HOT guys. A picture of Ryan flashed into her head, and she had to bite back a whimper. That last night with him... God, what a beautiful night that had been.

He didn't know it, but he'd fixed something for her. He'd made her less afraid. She didn't know why, but since she'd left his side early that morning, she hadn't been as scared of anything as she had been before. The only thing she'd been afraid of was leaving him. Having him hate her.

Her heart flipped and she swallowed. She'd wondered how he reacted when he got the news. She'd made Ian promise to send a message to Colonel Mendez. She didn't want Victoria and Ryan wondering if she'd been kidnapped or snatched by a serial killer or something. She needed them to know she was alive and had gone of her own free will.

But how had they reacted? Victoria would have been furious, of course. But what of Ryan? Was he angry, or disgusted?

She hated the idea that he might despise her, but there was no going back now. She only hoped that when this was all over, he might forgive her.

"Emily."

She stopped at the sound of Ian's voice. He came out of the shadows of his office door, his eyes raking over her. Dark eyes. Eyes filled with things she couldn't begin to fathom.

She liked Ian. She felt like he was a kindred soul somehow.

"Mustafa didn't show," she said, getting down to business. "He said the last time he might not be able to get away."

Ian blew out a breath. "Dammit. We need to figure out where they're holding those hostages."

"I know." She gritted her teeth. "Why haven't you sent me yet? I should be inside the cell, getting the information for us."

"You aren't ready."

Anger surged inside her. And frustration. "How much more ready can I be? I've been here for two months, Ian. I speak the language. I am the Light of Zaran," she spat, hating the name as much now as she did then. She hadn't been his light at all. He'd used it to mock her, mock that she'd come to mean nothing to him.

"It's not as simple as that. There's groundwork to be done. If you walk in there and they aren't prepared for it, they'll kill you. They have to believe that you've returned willingly, that you escaped the Americans and want to help their cause."

She snorted. "I was a part of their cause for three years. I think I can fake it well enough."

"We don't know who's in charge now. Since Al Ahmad was taken, things have changed. Your husband was slaughtered with his own knife, his men were overrun, and you disappeared. How do you think that looks?"

40

She felt herself pale, but she didn't shrink from his stare. Ian didn't know that she'd been the one to shove that knife into Zaran's gut. Or maybe he did and he just hadn't told her.

"It looks like I was kidnapped when they killed my husband and his men. How else is it supposed to look?"

"Like maybe you betrayed them?"

Her stomach roiled. "How it looks hasn't changed in the past two months. You knew this from the beginning, but you still brought me here. For what, Ian? To meet with Mustafa and pass on information someone else could have gotten?"

His gaze hardened. "I brought you here to do a job, which is what you're doing. You know these people. You know what they're like. Filtering the information from Mustafa—who wasn't nearly as forthcoming with anyone else as he has been with you, by the way—through the lens of your experience is invaluable to us. When the time is right, I'll send you in. Not a minute before. Besides, this situation with the hostages changes things a bit, at least for now."

Emily put her hand over her eyes and pressed against the tears threatening to fall. For heaven's sake, why was she so emotional? Did she really want to walk into a den of terrorists and pretend to be one of them? What she was doing now was dangerous enough. She met with her contact at a location of his choosing. She went alone. If he decided to grab her or if he fed her wrong information, how would she stop him?

There was always someone from Ian's group watching, but that didn't mean they could stop the man if he tried. He wasn't precisely trustworthy. Hassan Mustafa was a jaded warrior who'd grown tired of the promises and ideals of the group. He hadn't grown tired of the possibilities of padding his own pockets, however.

So he sold information to Ian, and then he went back to the group. How did she or Ian know he was telling them the truth? They didn't, not really, but it was true that a group of archaeologists had been kidnapped in the Lost City of Maz recently. The Freedom Force hadn't released any videos yet, but she knew it was coming.

She desperately needed Mustafa to tell her where they were being held so someone could get them out. She'd tried before, but he was reluctant to talk about it. He was afraid. She understood that, but her duty was to get him to talk. Maybe if they offered him more money. Everything was about money to Mustafa.

Emily straightened as a wave of weariness washed over her. "Rascal said something about company coming to help us with the archaeologists."

Ian's gaze darkened for a moment. "Hostage rescue, yes. The government is sending in a military team. Once we learn where the hostages are, they'll go in and extract them."

Her heart thumped. *A military team…* "Why can't we do that?"

He had enough men here. Enough equipment and expertise. Ian Black pretty much had his own army, so they didn't really need another one showing up.

"Not our mission. It requires too many resources and shifts focus off what I need to accomplish out here."

Frustration hammered her. "And just what is it you need to accomplish, Ian? I've never been clear on that."

"But I *am* clear, and that's all that matters." He shook

his head. "You're exactly like Victoria in some ways, and nothing like her in others."

Her skin prickled. She'd spent her life wanting to be as strong and confident as her big sister. She never had been. She'd been the weak one, the one who'd caused more trouble than she was worth. Victoria had always picked up the pieces for her. This time Emily wanted to pick up the pieces. She wanted to prove she was worth all the trouble and make her sister proud for a change.

She also wanted to make Ryan proud, though she knew that was probably a tall order considering how she'd left him.

"Victoria is the most amazing woman I know."

"She is. I'm glad she's found happiness." Ian's expression didn't change, but Emily detected a subtle shift in him.

Emily found herself staring at him as something she'd sensed finally crystallized in her mind. "You're in love with her."

His eyes glittered. "I'm not sure I know what that means."

But he did, deep down. She knew it by looking at him.

Emily put a hand on his arm. Squeezed. "It means I see the look in your eyes when you talk about her. There's regret, and maybe some pain. I'm an expert at that, you know."

He snorted, and she knew she'd hit the mark. It humanized him in a way nothing else had.

"Anything I *might* have once felt for your sister is pointless. She has Nick Brandon—and I don't think he's ever had trouble telling her what he feels."

Emily thought of the way Nick looked at her sister. She'd watched them a lot over the few months they'd been together, and she'd been envious. They had something she'd never had. Something she desperately wanted. Maybe everyone wanted it—but few seemed to get it.

"No, I don't think he does. They're right for each other. But whoever's right for you will come along someday, and then you'll never believe you thought you wanted someone else when that person exists."

He laughed. "You're a romantic, Emily."

She shrugged as heat flooded her cheeks. "I guess I am. It's probably what got me in trouble with Zaran. I thought he was a knight in shining armor. I know better now. I know real knights are practically nonexistent."

"Hey, boss," a voice interrupted from the entry. "The GIs are here. Group of 'em wants to see you."

"Let them in," Ian said before turning to her. "You might want to disappear for this. Mendez sent HOT. Victoria won't be with them, but I don't know who else might be. There's a chance you'll know some of them."

He said it so casually, like the neighbors were popping in for tea. But it was much worse than that to her. Emily's feet stuck to the floor. She wanted to move, wanted to melt into the shadows and disappear, but a part of her wanted to see who'd come even more.

Not Ryan. Surely not Ryan. HOT was a big organization, and Mendez had at least a hundred men. He wouldn't send Ryan's squad when he had others.

Booted feet pounded toward them. Somehow Emily found the strength to wrench herself away and up the stairs. She stopped on the darkened landing, her heart hammering, and watched as the men came into view. They were wearing native dress—white tunics with baggy pants and kaffiyehs on their heads to keep the sun from burning them to a crisp—but they were unmistakably American Special Operators to her.

She didn't recognize the first one she saw. He was tall and broad with a hard look in his eyes. Then she saw Matt Girard and her stomach twisted. Chase Daniels came into view.

The next man to step into sight made her slap her hand over her mouth to stop any sound from escaping. Ryan wore an ammunition belt slung around his waist, but the rifle was missing. She knew that whoever manned the entry would have made them all leave their weapons behind, and she was thankful for that at this very moment because violence simmered in the air around these men.

Ryan's pale blue eyes were hard in his tanned face, and his jaw was set in a formidable line. She'd never seen him look so angry. He was the funny one, the one who told jokes and didn't get rattled over anything. When other guys flew off the handle, Ryan said something that had everyone in stitches.

But that wasn't the Ryan she saw now. This was a Ryan she'd never seen before. He was a man on the edge of something.

One minute he was standing there, and then he moved so fast that she didn't see precisely what he did. No one else did either, because they failed to stop him. He'd been standing with his teammates, but now he had an arm wrapped around Ian's neck and a knife against his throat.

Ian stood in his grip as calmly as possible for a man who was seconds from death.

"Goddammit, Flash, put the knife down," Matt Girard

said. "That's a fucking order, soldier."

Ryan didn't obey. If anything, he looked angrier than before. "No, sir, I can't do that. Not until this piece of shit tells us where Emily is."

SIX

EMILY'S HEART THREATENED TO POUND right out of her chest. Ryan was here—and he was threatening Ian because of her.

Part of her wanted to run up the stairs and hide. And part of her wanted to fling herself into Ryan's arms.

Logically, she knew there would be no flinging. She knew he was murderously angry, and she knew she had to stop him before he did something irrevocable. Something that would be her fault.

"Ryan!" she shouted, stumbling down the stairs as the abaya twisted around her legs. She caught herself before she fell, grasping the edge of the wall and scraping her hand in the process.

Heads whipped around to look at her, but it was only Ryan she saw. His blue eyes clashed with hers, and she nearly recoiled from what was contained in them.

Anger. Hate. Relief.

And loathing. God, the loathing.

"I'm okay, Ryan," she said, her voice shaky, her stomach twisting and rolling as bile rose in her throat.

"Jesus, Flash, let the man go." Chase spoke this time. He held out a hand as if he were trying to calm a rabid dog. "She's here. She looks fine to me. This isn't what we're here for, and you know it."

Ryan didn't move for a long moment. And then he dropped his knife to his side and shoved Ian away. "I fucking know it," he growled. "But we have a result, don't we?"

Ian turned around and touched his throat. There was blood on his hand as he drew it away. His eyes sparked with fury, but he didn't do anything about it.

Emily was glad for that, because she knew that every man here was overloaded with testosterone and a hair-trigger temper at the moment.

"If you're going to attack a man with skills equal to yours, you need to kill him before he fucking kills you," Ian growled.

Ryan ignored him and advanced on her. Had he always been this big? This formidable? He towered over her, and his expression hadn't softened one bit. Her stomach bottomed out.

"You went willingly. After…" He shook his head, his jaw hardening as he gazed down at her. He practically vibrated with anger. "I can't believe you left like that. Do you know how worried Victoria's been? How worried we've all been?"

Emily lifted a hand, but he recoiled from her as if he couldn't bear for her to touch him. Hot tears pressed against her eyelids.

"I was trying to do the right thing—"

"The right thing?" He looked at her disbelievingly. "The right fucking thing wasn't leaving people who care about you! It wasn't leaving my bed in the middle of the night without a fucking word!"

She heard the clearing of throats and a muttered curse, and it hit her that he'd just revealed something that would have been better off kept secret. For *his* sake, not hers.

"Not here," she said fiercely. "Not now."

He took another step toward her until he was nearly pressing her into the wall. "When? Fucking when, Emily?"

"Don't yell at me!"

He stepped back, his nostrils flaring. He flexed his hands at his sides as if trying to work off some tension.

Emily's body quivered with adrenaline. Her head swam, and the heat inside her abaya intensified. Her stomach churned as bile rose in her throat. She put a hand on the wall as the buzzing in her brain grew stronger. Why couldn't she shake this feeling?

Ryan's expression changed. He didn't look angry now. He looked... concerned.

"Emily? What's wrong?"

"I... I... don't... know..."

He was the only thing she could see. Everything else faded until his face filled her vision. She felt his hands on her shoulders—and then she felt nothing at all.

"Emily!" Ryan caught her as she crumpled to the ground. Then he swung her up into his arms and whirled on the men standing there.

"In here," Ian Black said, pushing open a door and walking into a room.

Ryan followed on his heels. It was an office, but there was a mattress on one wall. Ryan sank down and gently placed Emily upon it.

"She needs water."

Ian pressed a cold bottle into his hand, and Ryan twisted off the cap before pouring some on his fingers and patting her face. Then he snatched the black head covering off and freed her hair. The golden mass was matted with sweat.

He pressed his fingers to her jugular and took her pulse. It was strong, but too fast.

"Take the abaya off," Black said.

Ryan wanted to growl at the man and tell him to go away, but he didn't have time to worry about anyone else. Instead, he peeled the fabric up Emily's body and then lifted her and brought it over her head. She was wearing a thin T-shirt, a pair of camouflage pants, and jump boots underneath. She had a waterskin strapped to her back, and she was armed with an HK45CT, which surprised him more than it should.

He'd never thought of Emily as a warrior, no matter that she'd lived with the Freedom Force for three years or that she'd been in battle the night she'd killed Zaran. Of course she would be weapons trained, but she was supposed to be separate from this violence, innocent and happy as she went about her life. That was how he thought of her.

Dammit, she wasn't supposed to be *here*.

Ryan removed the pistol and cleared the chamber before ejecting the clip. He set them on the table nearby before he proceeded to pat Emily down with more water. Someone shifted the fan that was in the room until it blew on her.

Emily moaned and Ryan stilled.

"Emily? What's wrong, honey? What can I do?"

She didn't answer, and he patted more water on her skin.

"What's wrong with her? You fucking chewed her ass out, dickhead," Ian Black said. "And I think you probably gave away more information about the two of you than you intended in the process."

"Shut up, Black," Ryan growled. "If she hadn't been here with you, you'd be dead."

Black snorted. "Really? Before you managed to torture her location out of me? This is why she couldn't tell you, asshole. That whole alpha-gorilla thing you have going must have scared her shitless when she thought about it."

"Stay out of this, motherfucker. If not for you, she wouldn't be here."

"Flash."

Ryan glanced up at his team commander. Matt wasn't looking too happy at the moment, but then again, nobody was.

"Emily made a decision to join him," Matt said. "And she's not the reason we're here."

Ryan could only blink. Not the reason? Maybe not, but now that he had her in his sights, he wasn't letting her out of them again.

"We can't leave her here. We can't leave her with *him*."

51

Black rolled his eyes. "If you want to find out where those hostages are, you'd damn well better leave her here. She's the one making contact, the one who's going to find out their location for us."

Ryan couldn't speak. Rage rolled through him. The kind of rage that made him want to smash something—or someone.

He was pissed at Ian Black. At Emily. At himself for being so stupid as to get involved with her in the first place. He'd convinced himself she was this helpless little thing who needed his strength and his friendship.

He'd let himself care, and that was the one thing he knew he shouldn't have done. Because caring made you vulnerable to hurt.

He stood and glared at Black. "You don't fucking care who you put in danger, do you? She had a life in DC, a life away from all this shit—and you brought her back into it. What did you promise her?"

Black didn't look the least bit apologetic. "A chance to clear her name."

Ryan took a step toward him, ready to pummel the man for lying to her. If it were possible, Mendez would have done it. Ian Black had lied for reasons of his own, but Ryan wasn't going to let him get away with it.

"Ryan."

Emily's voice was soft and shaky, but her eyes were open. She gazed up at him with glassy brown eyes, and he sank down on the mattress beside her, pushing her hair back off her forehead with a tender gesture. Too late, he realized what he was doing and dropped his hand away.

"I'm sorry," she said softly.

Her apology kicked him in the gut. "He lied to you,

Emily. He can't do what he said. You need to go home and go back to school."

She moved her head from side to side on the pillow. Telling him no. Rejecting him.

He stiffened.

"You and Victoria want to cocoon me in Bubble Wrap and keep me from living my own life. This is something I need to do. I'm not leaving until it's finished."

"It's not safe here for you. You know that."

"It's not safe for you either. For any of us."

Ryan got to his feet. She was a stranger to him in so many ways. The woman he thought he'd known—the soft, sweet, sometimes confused woman—was nowhere in evidence. This woman was determined and stubborn.

But so was he. He turned to Ian Black and Matt, who'd come into the room with them.

"We need to call Mendez and get her on the next transport out of here. She can't stay."

Matt didn't look happy. He also didn't look like he agreed, and that was enough to make Ryan nearly burst a blood vessel.

"Can't do nothing about it, *mon ami*," he said, his Cajun accent thickening for a second. "She's here and she doesn't want to go. Our mission is to extract the hostages, and that's what we're going to do."

Emily was sitting up now and holding a hand to her stomach. She didn't look as green as she had a few minutes ago, but she didn't look well either.

"She's sick. She needs medical attention."

"Stop talking about me like I'm not here," Emily said, her eyes blazing hot. "I'm not sick. It's just something that comes and goes. I got too hot. I'll be fine in a little while."

Matt frowned as he looked at her. Then his gaze landed on Ryan again. "You heard her, Flash. Now let's get down to the business we came here for, which is finding those hostages."

Ryan felt like he'd landed in an alternative universe. After two months of worrying about Emily, wondering where she was and if she was safe, he'd found her again. But she wasn't the same person. She didn't want his opinion. She didn't want to tell him her problems or listen to his advice the way she once had.

Two months ago, she'd come to him and said she had to be with him, just once. Said he was the brightest spot in her life. Then she'd snuck out of his apartment while he'd slept and she'd left the country with Ian Black. He'd felt betrayed, angry, confused.

He'd gotten a handle on those feelings in the past two months. But the lid had snapped off today, and everything was churning in his gut right now.

He'd told himself on the long flight here that he would find her again. That once he had Ian Black in his sights, he was getting an answer no matter what he had to do to get it.

But he hadn't expected to walk into Black's compound and find her with little effort. Hell, until a few minutes ago, he'd even let himself believe she wasn't here willingly. He'd believed she'd get on a plane as soon as he found her and go back to DC gratefully.

She didn't look grateful at the moment. She looked upset and miserable.

"I was just telling Ian that my contact didn't come to the rendezvous today," she said to Matt. She didn't look at Ryan, and it stung. "He's not ready to divulge that info yet. Not without more incentive."

"You aren't going out there again," Ryan said. "It's too dangerous."

All three of them looked at him. Matt's jaw was set in a hard line. Emily looked furious. Black was the only one with the hint of a grin on his face. Ryan wanted to wipe it away with a solid punch.

"I make the personnel decisions around here," Black said. "And I say she goes. Unless, of course, she decides she'd rather not. Emily?"

Her face was red as she lifted her chin. "I'm going. I'll try again tomorrow. I'll keep trying until we have an answer."

Black went over to his desk and fired up the combat-hardened laptop sitting there. "We're working with satellite imagery to try to find where they might be, but so far we don't have anything concrete to go on. There are some native tribes in the area that camp out in different locations—the Freedom Force could be with one of them, but we can't go blasting our way into every camp to look. If we do that and we have it wrong, the word will spread. We won't have a chance of getting those people back alive if that happens."

"Agreed," Matt said.

But Ryan couldn't get on board with the conversation. He was too invested in the fact that Emily had run away in the night and now she was ignoring him. It just didn't compute.

"So what was all that in my apartment?" he said. "Lies? Why bother? Why come to me with your bullshit about wanting to be with me?"

"Jesus," Ian Black said.

"Flash, not here, dude," Matt added. "Not now. I already have to tell the colonel—don't add fuel to the fire."

Emily dropped her gaze from his as she fiddled with the edge of the abaya lying on the mattress. He waited for her to look at him, but she didn't. And he suddenly knew he'd be waiting for a long fucking time. Whatever had happened between them in DC was over.

"Yeah, all right, I get it." He turned toward Matt. "Unless you need me for this, I'm going to go find my bunk or something."

Matt looked sympathetic, which didn't help soothe the bruised feeling in Ryan's chest.

"Go ahead. Tell the guys we'll meet in an hour."

"Copy that."

He didn't mean to look at her again, but like Lot's wife, he couldn't help himself. He didn't turn into a pillar of salt, but his heart felt like stone as he walked away.

SEVEN

EMILY WANTED TO GO UP to her room and hide after Ryan stormed out, but she didn't let herself do it. Instead, she listened to Ian and Matt discuss the Freedom Force and the possible scenarios in which they'd use the hostages.

"Will they make an example of them, Emily?"

She looked up to find the two men staring at her. As soon as she'd felt stable enough, she'd gone over to sit in a chair instead of on the mattress—Ian had a mattress in his office because he slept there. While it was a pretty sparse setup without any personal touches, it still felt too intimate to lie on his bed.

She cleared her throat. She felt much better than she had, at least physically. Her heart, however, still felt as if someone had stomped on it pretty hard. She could still hear the anger in Ryan's voice, still see the disillusionment on his face. He'd been furious with her, and then he'd been disgusted.

But she couldn't let that affect her. She had a job to do. People's lives depended on it.

"They don't have scruples, if that's what you're asking. Up until now, executing hostages and broadcasting it hasn't been their style. Bombs in public places, suicide missions—yes. But beheading people on camera is new territory. I don't think they would shrink from it necessarily. On the other hand, they may not want to be identified with the groups who are currently using that tactic."

"So we may have some time yet," Matt said.

"A little bit, yes. Just because they may not want to film an execution doesn't mean they won't kill the hostages and leave their bodies to be found somewhere as a message."

"That's what I'm afraid of." Matt put a hand to his forehead and rubbed. "Will they kill a pregnant woman?"

Emily blinked. "I… Yes, I'm pretty sure they would. Are you telling me one of the hostages is pregnant?"

Matt nodded. "Linda Cooper. She's thirty-one, married, and fifteen weeks pregnant. She was only supposed to be on the dig for the first two weeks, then she was returning to Italy where she teaches in the military adult education program at Aviano Air Base. Her husband is an Air Force major."

"Oh, God," Emily breathed. "If they figure that out…"

Ian and Matt looked grim. "Yeah," Matt said. "We have to get her out of there. We have to get them *all* out of there."

Emily put her hand to her belly automatically. That poor woman was pregnant and no doubt scared out of her mind. And then there was the deprivation she was likely suffering at the hands of the Freedom Force. The hostages were probably getting food and water because the terrorists couldn't demand things if they were dead, but it certainly wasn't the kind of regular nutrition a pregnant woman would need.

What if she was sick? Suffering from heat exhaustion and morning sickness? She would be miserable. Puking, fainting, tired all the time…

A cold chill rolled down Emily's spine. Those things sounded remarkably similar to how she'd been feeling lately.

Except that she couldn't be pregnant. It wasn't possible. She'd wanted to be once, back when she still cared about Zaran. Before he'd become a monster. Once he'd changed, she'd been more than thankful she couldn't get pregnant, even if it did infuriate him.

A wave of nausea swelled in her throat, and she swallowed it down again. No, she wasn't pregnant. Linda Cooper was.

But… when was her last period? Not since before she'd arrived in Acamar two months ago. Emily chewed her lip and thought back to the last time. It was about two weeks before she'd left DC.

Two weeks before she'd spent the night with Ryan. A fresh chill slid over her skin.

No. There was just no way. No freaking way.

It had been a while, yes—but there was the stress of travel and getting acclimated to the heat. Those things messed up a woman's natural cycle. She'd been through that before.

Her period should happen any day now. Any day.

And if it doesn't?

It will.

Besides, it wasn't like she could walk down to the

corner drugstore and buy a pregnancy test. Which was fine because she wasn't pregnant. Her period was coming.

"All right," Ian was saying. "Get your guys settled and let me work my contacts for a while. If I get anything, I'll let you know."

"We're going to get them out of there," Matt said. "So long as we all work together."

Ian looked up and met the other man's gaze. "That's my intention. I wouldn't have passed the information along the chain if it wasn't."

"The guys don't trust you."

Ian grinned. "I know. But you do."

Matt didn't say anything at first. Then he stuck out his hand. Ian clasped it, and they stood there looking at one another for a long moment.

"The jury's still out, *mon ami*. But I'll give you the benefit of the doubt until you prove me wrong."

Ian shrugged. "I'm on your side this time—but I won't be every time. That much is true."

Matt started to walk away, but then he stopped and frowned at Emily. She had to drag her thoughts back from the depths of her distraction.

"I don't pretend to know what's going on with you and Flash," he said, "but clearly there's more here than any of us knew about. You need to talk to him when you're both calmer. This can't get in the way of the mission."

"It's not going to."

His frown didn't abate, and she knew he wasn't appeased. "Flash is one of the most easygoing guys I know. I don't think I've ever seen him this pissed before, and that worries me. If he's distracted during a mission, that's not good for any of us. And if I have to remove him from the op, that's not good for him. You get what I'm saying?"

Emily swallowed. If he had to remove Ryan from the mission, he'd get sent back to DC—and the wrath of Mendez. He could lose his job over her. His career. The fewer issues he had with her being here, the better. "I get it."

Matt nodded. "Good. Talk to y'all later."

Once he was gone, Ian sat back and ran his hands through his hair before settling them on top of his head and staring at her.

"You didn't mention a romantic entanglement with a HOT operator. I could have made sure he wasn't on the team."

Emily's face was warm. "I didn't think it was anyone's business but mine and Ryan's."

"Maybe not, but he's here now, and you have to work with him. Are you going to be able to do that?"

Emily sniffed as if it was nothing when in truth her stomach was still churning, and not just from nausea. "Of course I am. It was just a brief fling."

She got to her feet and picked up the abaya, her fingers trembling from the lie. "If there's nothing else, I have some things to do."

Ian's eyes narrowed. "Nope, nothing else."

Ryan was lying on a bunk in the room he was sharing with Fiddler when Matt appeared in the doorway. He'd known his team commander would visit him, but he'd hoped it would take a bit longer. He was still processing everything that had happened with Emily, and he was still pretty pissed about it. His first instinct was to go find her and throw her over his shoulder like a caveman. Then he'd take her to the airstrip and load her onto a C-17 headed for Germany.

After the plane was gone, he *might* calm down, though he had no idea how long that would take. Days, at least.

So the last thing he wanted to do right now was answer questions about him and Emily, but he knew he had no choice. He was a soldier, the man frowning at him was his superior, and Ryan obeyed orders.

Matt came inside and sank down on the bunk opposite. "So, you and Emily. Care to explain?"

No dancing around the subject there. Ryan sat up and leaned against the wall. "Not especially."

Matt's gaze didn't falter. "You realize that isn't an option, right?"

"I do." He huffed out a breath. "There's not a lot to explain. She confided in me after the mission in Qu'rim. I didn't cut it off when I should have because I seemed to be the only person she could talk to…"

"And?" Matt prompted when he didn't keep talking.

Ryan felt his skin growing hot. Not because he was embarrassed but because he really didn't want to talk about what had happened in his apartment that night. It was personal. And while he might have talked shit in the past about getting a piece of pussy after a night in a club or something, it felt wrong to talk about Emily that way.

"Flash, I have to know."

Ryan scrubbed a hand over his scalp. "It was only once. The night before she left with Black. She'd tried to date a guy in her class, but it didn't work out. She needed to know if she was still capable of... She needed to know if she was normal. I didn't say no."

Matt nodded. "All right. Now explain to me why you lost your cool back there."

Ryan's throat was tight. "What's there to explain? Ian Black isn't trustworthy—and he lied to Emily to get her out here for his own reasons. He put her in danger, and she was stupid enough to believe him. She hurt Victoria by leaving—and Brandy too because he loves Victoria."

"And you. She hurt you too."

Fuck. He could deny it, but what was the point? "And me."

"I need to know if you're going to be able to do this job with her here. Because she's not leaving. Black isn't forcing her to stay, and she doesn't want to go. Not only that, she understands things about the Freedom Force that no amount of intel in the world can tell us. She lived with them, and she knows how they think."

Precisely why he wanted her gone. He didn't want her to have to endure those people again. To relive the hell she'd gone through with Zaran bin Yusuf. It had to be costing her something to be in such close proximity to the life that had nearly broken her once before.

"You don't care that Black lied to her?"

Matt's eyes sparked. "How do you know he did? Maybe he has the connections to do what he promised."

A flash of anger rolled through him. "Now *you* believe this motherfucker? After what he did when he sent Victoria and Brandy after that Russian scientist?"

"What did he do? He turned the virus over to us instead of selling it, which he could have done if he'd wanted. I don't like him or trust him, but I believe we're on the same side."

"We play by rules. Ian Black has no rules."

"Nope, I don't think he does either. He'll do whatever it takes to get what he wants, no matter how unscrupulous."

"Working with him is like teaming the police department with a vigilante group and giving them the same powers."

"Not gonna argue with you there. But this is the job, Flash. You know it as well as I do. Mendez sent us here to get a job done, and we're going to do it. Those people out there who are scared and in danger—they take precedence over any feelings we have for Black. They also take precedence over this situation between you and Emily. I need you to be in control of your feelings about this."

"I am in control. How many missions have we done together? Have I ever failed the team in all that time?"

"No, but a woman can have a way of fucking with a guy's head."

Ryan closed his eyes and rolled his neck. "She's not fucking with my head. I was surprised and pissed. I'll get over it."

Matt leaned forward, his palms on his knees. "I have to report this to the colonel, but unless you give me a reason to remove you now, I'll wait until the mission is over. The safety of the hostages takes priority."

Ryan hated that the overwhelming feeling coursing through him at the mention of Mendez was relief that Matt wasn't telling the colonel yet. He'd have to face the music eventually, of course, but he was glad it wasn't today. Even half a world away, the colonel was one badass, scary motherfucker. Ryan didn't know what it was like to be on the man's bad side, and he didn't want to find out.

Though he suspected this situation between him and Emily would push his relationship with the colonel into the danger zone. Mendez didn't like surprises, and he certainly didn't like having to clean up messes made by his own men.

"I'll do my job, Richie. Like always."

Matt stood and nodded. "Knew I could count on you." He looked down at his watch. "Team meeting in twenty."

"I'll be there."

EIGHT

MENDEZ SAT IN HIS OFFICE, poring over reports. It was already dark and he'd been at work since before dawn, but that's the way his days typically went. He didn't have much time for a personal life.

Didn't need much time for one either. About the only thing he required from his life that he didn't get from HOT was sex, and he found time for that, though perhaps not as often as he might like. In fact, the last time... Shit, he couldn't remember the last time. A month ago? Two months?

There was a knock on his door.

"Enter."

His aide came into the room. "Sir, I wanted to check if you needed anything before I left."

Mendez stretched and looked at the clocks on the wall. There was one for every time zone in the world, but the biggest one was for the eastern US. When he realized what time it was, he stood. "Lieutenant, you should have been gone two hours ago."

The young man smiled. "Yes, sir, but I wanted to stay

in case you needed me."

"Go home." Mendez shoved some papers into his briefcase. Then he took the classified reports and his hard drive and put them in the safe before closing it and spinning the dial. "I'll walk out with you."

Once in the parking lot, Mendez climbed into his SUV and headed for home. But when he got there, he couldn't make his mind rest. If the Freedom Force executed those hostages, there would be hell to pay.

Aside from the fact he didn't want to let those bastards harm innocent civilians, he also didn't want to have to field questions from senators charged up over an incident and looking to make an example of someone for letting it happen. HOT was always one vote away from a funding cut, as were most organizations these days.

And he believed too much in what they were doing to see that happen.

When it became apparent he wasn't going to quiet his thoughts anytime soon, he changed into jeans and a polo shirt and headed for a bar he liked. Not Buddy's, where his men hung out, because he knew that seeing him meant they couldn't relax. He was the boss, and having the boss around tended to dampen their enthusiasm.

It was part of being in charge, so he was used to it. Besides, most of his guys were in their twenties and early thirties. He was pushing fifty, though not quite there yet—but he still felt old when compared with them, even if he could do more push-ups than many of them. He'd gotten into the habit of challenging them at work from time to time. Kept him on his toes, and kept them surprised when he won most of the battles.

They might respect his rank and his power as their

commander, but by God, he also wanted them to respect him as a warrior.

He parked under a streetlight and walked into the bar. It was an upscale kind of place, which was another reason he chose it. Less likely to get into scrapes in a joint where the beer was craft and the wine fancy. No cheap beer and free snacks here. No pool games or darts either, which was a shame in some respects.

Mendez went inside and found a table in a dark corner. He could see all the doors from back there, and he could react if someone invaded the place. Not that it was likely, but he'd seen enough combat to always be prepared.

He scoped out the entrances and exits of every establishment he entered, and he chose the best spot from which to defend his position if necessary. He was armed, though in a bar it had to be a knife rather than a gun if he was complying with local law. Still, he could do a lot of damage with a knife. More so than the average thug, that's for sure.

The waitress came over, and he ordered a local brew before sitting back and watching the patrons. The interior was dark, and the people were much quieter than in some of the other places he'd been. It was downright civilized.

He was beginning to think he'd chosen wrong this time—that he needed more action and stimulation—when the door opened and a woman walked in.

A woman he recognized. Every cell in his body went on red alert at the sight of Samantha Spencer. She was medium height, medium build, with the kind of curves that didn't quit, golden-blond hair tied in a ponytail, and only a minimum of makeup. She wore a black dress that hugged those curves and thin heels that showed her legs to perfection when she walked. She was carrying a small red purse.

A man came over and kissed her on the cheek. He'd been aiming for her mouth, but Sam turned her head at the last minute, and his lips met her cheek instead. She said something then, her expression amused, and the man offered his elbow.

She took it, and he led her toward a table opposite from where Mendez sat. He wondered if her date knew what she did for a living. Sam was, without doubt, one of the smartest and toughest CIA agents he'd ever known. She wasn't in the field anymore, according to what he'd heard. She'd returned a few months ago from the Middle East and taken a desk job at Langley in the intel division.

He hadn't seen her in years, but that didn't stop his body from tightening with memories. They'd been Army officers together once. And they'd been lovers.

It hadn't worked out.

The waitress delivered his beer, and he picked up his phone to scroll through e-mail as he tried to shake off old memories. Old regrets.

"Drinking alone, Johnny?"

He looked up to find Sam standing beside his table. Damn her for moving so quietly that he hadn't even noticed. He set the phone down and stood to greet her. A quick glance at her date told her the guy was immersed in his tablet and unconcerned that she'd walked over to talk to him instead.

"I like drinking alone." He took the hand she offered and clasped it gently. A sizzle of attraction rolled through him at that simple touch. And suddenly he found himself doing something he shouldn't with this woman. He stepped to her side and gave her a kiss on the cheek.

Her skin was soft, her hair smelled like flowers, and his groin stirred as she gasped softly. He still remembered what it had felt like to sink into her, even after so many years.

"It's good to see you, Sam," he murmured as he stepped back again.

Her hand was still clasped in his as she blinked at him. Then she pulled it away, and he missed the warmth of her skin on his.

"It's been a while."

"About five years, I imagine."

Her eyes sparkled with humor. "Something like that. It was a briefing in Germany. You were annoyed with the major giving the presentation."

He laughed. "He was a posturing asshole."

"And when you were done with him, he was probably just an asshole on his way to a new, less than cushy assignment."

"Something like that."

He wondered what she knew about Ian Black since she'd spent so much time in the Middle East bureau and must surely know him—or know *of* him—but now certainly wasn't the time to ask.

Though Black operated outside the bounds of the law much of the time, it was clear to Mendez after the mission with Grace Campbell that Black was still working with the CIA even though they denied it. Which made Mendez very curious about a lot of things, not the least of which was the identity of the agent running Black.

Whoever it was had to be highly placed and utterly secretive. Though Mendez wasn't sure that Black's handler had as much control over him as they thought they did. Black seemed to be willing to work for the highest bidder, though he also did the right thing when the principle was inviolable.

The man was definitely an enigma.

"I have to get back to my date," Sam said, throwing a glance over her shoulder. "But I wanted to say hi."

Mendez let his gaze drift back to the man who was now watching them with narrowed eyes. "He your boyfriend?"

Sam laughed. "If I didn't know better, I'd think that question had a touch of jealousy in it."

"Maybe it does," he said, and she lifted an eyebrow.

She shrugged. "He's not my boyfriend. He's someone a friend set me up with. A meddling friend who thinks I work too much and don't get out enough."

"Work doesn't keep you warm at night."

Her mouth curled in a smile. "Ah, Johnny, that's ironic coming from you."

"Probably is."

She shook her head. "You are remarkably flirtatious this evening, aren't you?"

"I'm a man, Samantha. I appreciate a beautiful woman when I see one."

"Oh, I do know that about you. Your *appreciation* was quite intense, if I remember rightly."

He was glad it was dark because he was suddenly, instantly hard. "I was an idiot back then. I should have appreciated you more."

Her hazel eyes softened. "Well, I really should get back to my date. Maybe I'll see you around."

He tried not to be disappointed. He deserved her indifference. What did he expect after all these years? "Maybe so."

She turned and went back to her table. Her date stood at her approach, his face wreathed in smiles that Mendez hated on sight. The man took her hand and helped her into the booth, then shot Mendez a glare when Sam dug in her purse for something. He glared right back until Sam spoke and the man had to turn his attention to her instead.

Mendez sat down and took another drink of his beer. But for the next hour, he couldn't tear his gaze—or his thoughts—from Samantha Spencer.

NINE

BY EVENING, EMILY FELT MUCH BETTER. Her spells usually came on in the morning and then here and there throughout the day, but by evening she typically felt fine. Yet another thing she had in common with a pregnant woman.

Emily frowned as she stared at herself in the mirror. *You are not pregnant.*

No, she wasn't. But now that she knew Linda Cooper was, she couldn't seem to stop thinking about it. That poor young woman. Her poor baby.

Emily splashed water on her face and took her hair down to brush it and then wind it up into a fresh bun. She secured it with a few bobby pins, blew out a breath, and looked herself over with a critical eye.

She hadn't worn makeup since she'd returned to the desert, but she wished she had some right now. Because no matter how much she might like to avoid Ryan, she was pretty sure she'd see him again. Most likely when she went to get her dinner. She could probably get someone to bring her something, but that was too cowardly even for her.

Everyone in this compound was a soldier, a person who'd chosen to be here and work hard for a cause. There was a cook and a supply clerk, just like in the Army, and whatever other positions Ian had hired out—but there were no maids or waitstaff.

They sent the linens out for cleaning, but they made their own beds if they had one—some of the guys bedded down in sleeping blankets. They also went to the dining room at mealtimes and got their own food.

Emily closed her eyes and put her hands on either side of the sink. She could do this. She *would* do this. She'd never thought Ryan would show up when she'd taken Ian's offer two months ago, but maybe she should have realized it could happen.

Naïvely, she'd thought maybe what Ian wanted from her would really only take a couple of weeks or so, and then she'd be home again before she'd damaged her relationship with Ryan and Victoria too badly.

"That's the kind of thinking that always gets you in trouble, Em," she muttered. Since she'd been a child and she and Victoria went into foster care, she'd had an inner fantasy life that often didn't dovetail with her reality.

When the twenty-five-year-old son who still lived at home in one of their foster families paid special attention to her, she'd only been fourteen and she'd been desperate for love and attention. She hadn't thought it wrong that he gave her that attention, even when it involved initiating her into sexual life far earlier than she should have been.

Oh, the things she'd told herself. The lies.

Of course it crumbled, and of course they were sent away to another family and then another and another. Victoria hadn't understood it, but Emily had. It was her. She was the bad one, the disappointment, the one who ruined everything.

That's when she'd turned to drugs and alcohol. They made her feel better, if only for a little while. She hadn't believed she could turn into an addict, but she had. That's what cocaine did. Thank God it had only been cocaine and not meth. She'd been terrified of meth, and that had saved her.

At least until Zaran found her. He'd been an addiction of another kind, though she hadn't realized it at first. She'd only wanted to please him. She'd done everything to please him—and he'd turned on her.

Everyone turned on her eventually.

"No," she hissed, staring at her reflection with glittering eyes. "That's not true."

Victoria hadn't turned on her. Men might come and go, but her sister would always love her.

Emily dashed the tears from her cheeks and patted her face with a towel before grabbing her weapons. She checked her .45 and holstered it, then slipped her knives into the ankle and belt sheaths designed for them.

If the Freedom Force came after her, she'd fight back. She'd die fighting back if she had to. Never again would she allow others to harm her.

Emily went downstairs and crossed the compound toward the dining area. She held her chin high as she stepped into the room. Men looked up from the groups in which they sat. She crossed over to the table where the cook dished chicken and rice onto a plate for her. She took it and went to join a group of men she knew.

Rascal made room for her, and she sat down and picked up her fork. She could feel eyes on the back of her head though. Her scalp tingled, and her fingers trembled as she fumbled the fork.

"You still not feeling better, Em?" Rascal asked, his brow pleating in concern.

"I'm all right. It's just noisier in here than usual."

Rascal shot a look across the room. "Yeah. Eighteen military operators make a difference."

"Two teams then."

He lifted an eyebrow in approval. "Yep, two teams. Guess Uncle Sam wants those hostages back pretty bad."

"No one deserves what will happen to them if they aren't freed," she said softly.

"No, no one does."

"Emily?"

A chill went over her and she looked up. Her sister's fiancé, Nick Brandon, stood there, looking cool and casual and somehow murderous at the same time.

Great.

"Hi, Nick."

He grabbed a chair and turned it, straddling it so he could face her. "You okay?"

"Yes, I'm fine."

"You're here because you want to be?"

"Yes." She swallowed and set her fork down. She wasn't so hungry now. "I'm sorry I skipped out like that, but Victoria would have tried to stop me. You know that."

"I know she went through hell to find you the last time. I know what it cost her."

"Hey, man, don't guilt the girl." Rascal was looking kinda pissed. "I worked with Victoria for a couple of years. Girl is tougher than hell. Or was until you showed up. Speaking of which, I ain't forgot that you lied to us.

76

Tried to pretend you were some kind of asshole that'd been kicked out of the Army and wanted to join up with us. All you wanted was to take us down."

Nick's gaze slanted to Rascal. "I did my job, Rascal. Same as you. And you're still here, right? Nobody got taken down."

"If you two could stop the pissing contest," Emily said. They looked at her with expressions ranging from amused to annoyed. "Nick, I'm sorry, but I had to do what I had to do. Victoria *has* paid for caring about me, and I'm here to fix that. She'll never stop worrying about me, never stop blaming herself for being unable to get my life back for me with no strings attached. When I can't fly out of the country, she'll blame herself. When I can't get a government job, or any job that requires a security clearance, she'll blame herself. When I have to tell a man who might want to marry me that his life will change if he stays with me, Victoria will blame herself when he leaves me because he doesn't want to take that chance. If Ian can change that—if he can give me back what I lost when I married Zaran—then I'm going to seize the opportunity with both hands and make things right. Because I don't want Victoria to live her life thinking she failed me somehow."

Nick's expression didn't change. He still looked tough and mean and angry. And then he swiped a hand over his face and huffed out a breath. "All right."

Emily blinked. "All right? That's it?"

He nodded. "Yep. You hurt her when you left again, but I understand why you did it. I can't argue with that kind of motive because I'd do anything to make her happy too. Even when it pisses her off at first."

Emily blinked back tears. Jeez, she was emotional lately. "You're the best thing that ever happened to Victoria. If she doesn't tell you that ten times a day, she's crazy."

Nick's smile was sudden. "Don't worry, I remind her when she's slacking in Nick-worship." He reached out and took her hand, squeezed it gently. "I hope like hell Ian gives you what he promised, because you deserve it. If he doesn't, then I guess I get to kick his ass after all. Something I'd enjoy immensely, I might add—but I'd rather he keep his promise."

Nick got up and went back to his table. Emily pushed food around her plate, the back of her neck still tingling in warning.

"There's a guy over there staring at you like you took away his favorite toy. Want me to put a stop to it?"

Emily glanced up at Rascal. He was looking protective and furious, and she patted his arm. "No, it's fine. He's angry with me for good reason. If he can't glare at me, he'll probably explode."

Rascal tipped his chin toward her plate. "You better eat something, girlie. Shoving it around the plate won't do you any good when you need the energy."

"My stomach is still off, I think."

Rascal stood and went over to the cook's table. When he came back, he had a big piece of warmed flatbread. He set it down next to her plate. "Eat the bread then. It'll help."

Emily's heart hitched as she tore off a piece of the bread and put it in her mouth. Rascal was a good guy, almost motherly in a way, and she liked him. He'd never, not once, made her feel like she didn't belong or like he wanted anything more from her than conversation once in a while. He'd never made a pass at her, and she appreciated that more than she could say.

Emily finished the bread, then sat and listened to Rascal and the other guys razz each other and tell stories. The dining room quieted as men filtered away, and still she sat. She knew Ryan was in the room because she could feel him looking at her.

Finally she turned and met his gaze. He was sitting alone now, leaning back against the wall, his hand around a cup on the table. Her heart flipped at the sight of him. She had a strong urge to go over and beg him to forgive her, but she knew she'd gone too far to ask him for that.

Still, she stood and went to where he sat. His eyes were hooded as she approached. Her stomach churned and her pulse throbbed as she stopped in front of the table.

I love you, her heart whispered. *I need you.*

No. No more need. No more vulnerability because she wanted love. She couldn't go down that path again. She loved Ryan Gordon with everything she had in her, but she wasn't about to beg him to love her in return. And how could he after the way she'd lied to him?

"I didn't expect to see you out here," she said. "Maybe I should have, but I didn't."

His eyes glittered hot. "This is the job, Emily. If there's danger, then you should expect me to turn up. Especially when it involves the Freedom Force."

She slid into a seat opposite him. "I had hoped to be back before now."

He snorted. "That's the problem with covert ops, honey. You never know what's going to happen."

Her ears were hot. "Ian didn't lie to me. He gave me a chance to clear my name in ways that HOT didn't offer. Maybe Victoria didn't want me to get involved with this kind of work and made sure Mendez didn't offer, or maybe Mendez just doesn't have that kind of influence." She shrugged. "It doesn't matter anymore, because I'm here— and my knowledge is useful."

He took a sip from the cup. She noticed his knuckles were white.

"You should have told me."

She snorted. "Would you have let me go?"

His jaw tightened. "No, probably not."

"Exactly."

"I didn't realize anything was wrong at first," he said, his tone conversational. "I woke up and you were gone. No big deal. Maybe you had class. Maybe you were protecting me. But I knew I'd hear from you later, so I didn't worry about it."

There was a knot in her stomach. "Ian said I couldn't communicate with anyone once I got on the plane. So I didn't."

"I texted you that afternoon. Still didn't worry when you didn't immediately reply. But that night, when I hadn't heard a word all day? Yeah, I began to get concerned. That's when I drove to your place and your roommate told me you hadn't been there all day. I searched your room. There wasn't much missing, but there was enough to tell me you'd gone somewhere. Somewhere warm judging by the clothes you didn't take."

"Ian sent a message."

"The next day, after I spent a night trying to piece together where you could have gone. I didn't want to alarm

Victoria, but I called her and Nick. They didn't sound upset, so I knew they didn't know. I didn't tell them. Maybe I should have, but I didn't."

Her heart throbbed as she imagined him looking for her.

"I thought I did something to you, Emily. Something that made you run. Until the next morning when Mendez rolled in like a thunderstorm and pulled Victoria aside." His voice was hard, brutal. "I didn't even have a fucking right to know what he told her, yet I was the one who knew you were gone. Thankfully she didn't keep the information from the rest of us."

She wanted to reach for him, but she couldn't. She knew he wouldn't welcome her touch. Her eyes were blurry and she reached up to swipe away the tears. Damn, she was usually better at controlling herself than this, but these days she cried at the slightest provocation.

Not that this was slight at all. It was huge.

"You didn't make me run. I've told you why I did it. I won't keep apologizing." She dashed the tears away. "Do you know how many times I had to sit and wait for news from you? How many missions you went on while I worried and wondered?"

"It's not the same fucking thing. You knew what I did. You *knew*."

"It is the same! You're a Special Operator, and you do what you do to protect our country and its citizens. Well, I got asked to do the same, so here I am. You have no right to deny me the chance to help my country or to clear my name. I couldn't even *be* with you, Ryan. Not openly, not for your sake. And maybe you didn't want that anyway, but at least after this I would know it was because

81

of me and not because of something stupid I did in my life."

TEN

RYAN BLINKED. SHE THOUGHT HE wouldn't want to be with her?

God, all he could do was sit here and swallow down the need flooding him like a nuclear shock wave. Because he did want her, even if he was pissed as hell at her. And he didn't fucking care if she'd been married to a terrorist. He wanted to wrap her body around his and explore to his heart's content.

Once hadn't been nearly enough.

"If the fact you'd been married to bin Yusuf meant a damn thing to me, I wouldn't have kept talking to you in the first place." He leaned forward, searched her gaze with his. He knew he looked hard and angry, but he didn't have the ability to be anything else right now. "I encouraged you to find someone more like you. Someone who wasn't a part of this fucking life. You didn't need this shit again, yet you're in it and I fail to understand why you'd even begin to think that was okay."

Her eyes widened. And then color flooded her face. "Goddamn you, Ryan." She slapped a hand to her chest. "*I* make my own choices, all right? You don't get to make them for me. And what the hell does that mean, someone more like me? A damn basket case? Someone scared of their own shadow like I was?"

He didn't miss that she said *was*. Jesus, he didn't understand her at all. Who was this woman?

"It means someone normal, Emily. Someone who doesn't live on the edge of disaster as a means of earning a living. You deserve the picket fence, a guy who worships you and who'll be there for you every night. You deserve better than what you had before, and you deserve better than someone like me."

She snorted. "Listen to you. What made you ever think I wanted a picket fence? When did I say that?"

"You didn't have to say it. I saw you that night, when you were covered in his blood and suffering from shock. It would have never happened if you'd been back in the States, going to college, meeting some nice frat boy there and getting married."

Emily gaped at him, then shook her head. "You're kidding, right? Don't you watch the TV when you're Stateside, Einstein? How many *perfect*"—here she did air quotes—"*marriages* end up on the nightly news? How many unsolved murder shows are there on TV about relationships gone sour? You aren't living in reality if you think the same thing couldn't have happened to me in the States. No one is safe."

He gripped the cup so hard he thought he might break it. Finally he shoved it away and took a deep breath. How did she do this to him? How did she twist him up inside so thoroughly and make him uncertain which way was up?

He'd thought he knew her. He'd thought he knew

who she was and what she needed, but he was finding out he hadn't known a goddamn thing. Because she hadn't been truthful with him. She'd come crying to him so many times over the past few months, but here she was as strong as he'd ever seen her. Confident and certain.

"You aren't the person I thought I knew."

"I *am* the same, Ryan. You just can't see it because you're angry." She put her hands on the tabletop, clenched them together and looked at him earnestly. "I'm trying to fix my life, fix what I did wrong. Am I scared? Hell, yes. But that doesn't mean I'm quitting. I can't quit because I want the life I should have had. I want the freedom and the choice—and I want to save Linda Cooper and her baby."

She pushed back and stood. Their gazes locked for a long moment—and then she turned and walked away.

Emily woke up sick the next morning. Her stomach churned and sent her running straight for the bathroom. Once there, she threw up what little was in her stomach. Then she rinsed her mouth with water and stared at herself in the mirror.

Had she gotten some kind of crud? No one else was sick in the compound, but she didn't suppose that meant she couldn't be. She went out into the city often enough to come into contact with a bug.

She turned on the shower and got under the spray, hoping it would help settle the nausea a little bit. Her breasts were tender when she ran her hands over them and she winced. What the fuck?

Linda Cooper flashed through her mind, and Emily gritted her teeth. *Not pregnant, not possible.*

She'd seen a doctor, a Qu'rimi man who hadn't been very nice but had been perfectly competent. He'd said something about scarring on her tubes and impossible for an egg to get through, etc., etc. She'd had the report in her hand, and she'd gotten into the car Zaran had sent her in and gone back to their home crushed and weepy.

She didn't need to relive that moment to know how wrong it was to even attempt comparing her symptoms. Not to mention, no matter how much the thought of a dark-headed copy of Ryan might make her heart clench with longing, it most certainly wasn't something he would want to deal with when all they'd had was a one-night stand.

Especially not with the way he'd looked at her last night—like she'd betrayed him.

Emily finished her shower, then dressed, gasping when her hand brushed the side of her breast as she dragged on her T-shirt. She strapped on her weapons, slicked her hair into a wet ponytail, and gathered her courage before going downstairs.

She found Ian in his office. There was no one else with him at the moment. He looked up from his laptop as she entered.

"You look green," he said, frowning.

Emily sighed. "I know. Everyone keeps telling me."

He snapped the laptop closed. "I'll have Jared check you out."

Jared was one of the medics Ian kept on the payroll.

But he was more than a medic, having been an Air Force Pararescueman. He was as badass as any Special Operator, but with medical skills that were vital to a forward-based unit such as this.

And Emily absolutely did not want to see him. She didn't want anything to interfere with her mission here, especially now that Ryan had arrived. If she had a sniffle, or a stomach flu, he'd insist she needed evacuating. Emily didn't think Ian would cave in to that demand, but she didn't want to watch the two of them go head-to-head again.

"No, it's fine. I probably ate something."

Ian's eyes narrowed. "I can't risk you passing something to others around here." He picked up his cell phone and tapped in a message.

"I have to meet with Mustafa today. You aren't going to pull me, are you?"

Ian looked up. "Can you manage it?"

Emily swallowed a wave of nausea. "Of course. Who else is there? Besides, he trusts me."

"It's getting more dangerous," Ian said. "Mustafa is unpredictable, paranoid. And he knows who you are."

Emily shrugged, though she didn't particularly feel dismissive. It's just that she couldn't dwell on the danger if she was going to do this job right.

"He's known that for a while. I would think if he'd planned to betray me in some way, he'd have done it by now. The longer he talks to me, the worse it looks for him if anyone finds out."

Ian nodded. "That's certainly true. Still, I don't like how he's been stringing you along lately. He knows where the hostages are."

Emily had been thinking about that. "But what if he doesn't? He could just want us to think he knows so we'll keep paying him."

"It's possible. But his information in the past has always checked out."

"Yes, but he could have pissed someone off. Maybe they're suspicious of him."

Ian frowned. "If they are, that's not good for you, Emily. They'll be watching him."

"I'll take extra security then. They won't grab me in a public marketplace in broad daylight."

"I'm going with you."

Emily's head swung toward the door at the same time Ian's did. Ryan was silhouetted there along with Chase Daniels. They filled the wide entryway as if it were nothing. Shoulder to shoulder, they were big and intimidating in native dress instead of their typical military camouflage.

"Eavesdropping is a bad habit, fellas," Ian said.

Ryan walked into the room. "Funny coming from a spy."

Ian shrugged. "Pays the bills."

Emily rolled her eyes. "Both of you, stop."

Because she knew it wouldn't take much to set these two at each other's throats. Ryan hated Ian for bringing her out here. And Ian just plain didn't like anyone who let their emotions cloud their thinking. He was the ultimate *Star Trek* Vulcan in some respects—or so she'd have thought if not for the chink in his armor concerning her sister.

"I'm going." Ryan's tone brooked no argument.

Emily got to her feet and faced him. How had she ever thought he was easygoing and fun? He'd been there for her so often, and he'd never judged. But now?

Holy shit, now he couldn't seem to turn off the Judgey McJudge thing he had going on. It pissed her off.

"You aren't going, Ry. I've been doing this without you for nearly two months, and I don't need you guard-dogging me now. You'll compromise the mission."

His eyes widened. "Seriously? Do you have any idea who you're talking to? I live for the mission, sweetheart. And I've never compromised one yet."

"I already have a partner on this—"

"You said you were taking extra security. It's me and Chase, or you aren't going."

Her blood pressure had to be off the charts by now. Maybe if she walked over and punched the daylights out of him, she'd feel better. More likely, she'd break her hand in the process, and then she'd have to suffer for a split second of satisfaction.

"You are not the boss of me." It sounded so childish when she said it—and yet there it was. She was furious.

His jaw hardened. "You've made that clear, Emily. But I'll be damned if I let you go out there without some real backup."

She glanced at Ian, certain he'd be pissed at that slight to his guys, but he merely shrugged. Then he waved a hand.

"Take them. It'll free up the guys for some other stuff around here."

Not the answer she'd been expecting. But Ian did what he wanted, and right now he didn't want to fight with Ryan about this.

Emily stalked toward the door. Ryan didn't move, so she pushed him out of the way. Chase stepped back and held up both hands as if he were scared of her. Of course he wasn't, but at least he recognized a pissed-off woman when he saw one.

Now if only Ryan were half so smart...

ELEVEN

EMILY WENT STRAIGHT TO THE supply room and grabbed a freshly laundered abaya. She jerked it on with angry movements and then went to find David, the operative who usually shadowed her when she met with Mustafa.

He was in the dining area, finishing up breakfast. Emily plopped down beside him, ignoring her silent watchdogs as she did so. David looked up, his gaze going from one to the other and then over to her for an answer.

"Extra security," she said, reaching for a piece of toast and nibbling a corner. It didn't make her stomach turn, so that was good. She turned around to look at the men standing behind her. Ryan looked militant. Chase simply looked resigned. And they both looked imposing. "We aren't leaving for another hour," she said. "You might as well sit down. Or go polish your weapons."

"Not letting you out of my sight, Emily," Ryan practically growled.

Her heart bumped. She knew what he didn't say—that he didn't trust her not to go without him.

And truthfully, she couldn't say she wouldn't prefer it that way. But she wasn't stupid, and Ryan and Chase were HOT, which meant something. Definitely not a bad pair to have at your back when meeting with a terrorist.

When it was time to go, they headed out to the street. David had briefed them both on procedure, and she was glad to see that they'd blended into the crowds on the street as they followed her through the city to the market.

It was early enough that the heat wasn't oppressive, but she was still uncomfortable. And she'd been so mad she'd forgotten to strap on her waterskin. It wasn't standard procedure since she wasn't going out into the desert, but she liked to have water on her because of how ill she'd been lately.

She'd just have to wait until they reached the market and she could get a bottle of cool water from a vendor.

It took about fifteen minutes, but she finally reached the small café where Mustafa had dictated this meeting should take place. She'd come yesterday and he hadn't shown, but perhaps he would today.

Emily took a seat at the rear of the shop and watched the street. The café and market were open-air, and sweat trickled down her brow in spite of the overhead fans whipping at high speed.

The proprietor brought her a bottle of water and a small coffee, though the minute the strong scent invaded her nostrils, her stomach turned. She pushed it aside and took a sip of the water.

She scanned the street, but there was no sign of Mustafa. And no sign of David, Ryan, or Chase either. She had to admit she was comforted knowing they were there, even if she'd rather it was someone other than Ryan.

They'd been friends, but they clearly weren't anymore. That grieved her, though she couldn't spend too much time worrying about it. What was done was done. He might forgive her when this was all over, though maybe she'd be so angry with him she wouldn't care if he did.

He certainly had a way of pissing her off.

A man crossed the square and made his way toward the café. He wore white robes, and his face was covered. Her heart kicked up as she recognized the familiar stride of Hassan Mustafa. Relief and fear crashed through her now that he was here. What if he didn't tell her anything about the hostages? What if he was merely toying with her and trying to get more money out of Ian?

He'd told her once that he wasn't a true believer. "Like you were," he'd said, "I am with them for reasons other than the cause."

"Why stay?" she'd asked. "Why not get out while you can?"

His expression had changed, grown angry. "It is not so easily done. And I am a poor man. I need money to escape."

And he was getting that money from Ian. Mustafa came inside and made straight for her table. It was slightly alarming since he tended to be more cautious when he approached, but he simply plopped down and motioned to the waiter, who immediately brought a coffee.

Something had happened, but she didn't know what. Or maybe he was just growing tired of the game.

"You didn't come yesterday," Emily said in the Qu'rimi dialect she'd learned from Zaran.

"I could not leave my duties. And I will probably not be back after today, not for a while."

Her heart thumped. "Why not? Is something happening? Are they moving the hostages?"

His gaze sharpened. "It has been mentioned, yes."

"Where are they being held?"

He shrugged. "This I do not know… but I may know where they are going."

Emily's stomach churned. "And where is that?"

"There is a camp outside Ras al-Dura. You know it?"

Emily swallowed. Yes, she knew the camp. And Mustafa knew that she knew. It was the place in Qu'rim where HOT had found her and where she'd killed Zaran. Not that Mustafa knew that part, of course.

"That's rather far to take a group of American hostages, isn't it?"

His eyes gleamed black. He might not be a true believer, but he had no love for Americans. "Not when you wish to make an example of them."

Emily caught herself clutching the fabric of her abaya in the fist she'd made beneath the table. "And when will they be moved?"

Mustafa took a sip of his coffee. "In a few days."

Emily's throat felt tight. "It would really help if you knew where they were being held."

"And yet I do not."

Emily leaned in as frustration knotted into a ball in her belly. "Why not? Are you out of favor? Do they suspect something?"

A flash of anger crossed his features before he was able to mask it. He took his pipe from his tunic and tapped it on the ashtray. "You forget yourself, Light of Zaran. I owe you nothing, certainly not an explanation."

Emily's gut twisted as she thought of Linda Cooper

being held captive. The woman was no doubt scared half to death. She had a husband and a baby on the way, and right now she didn't know if she would live to see her baby born.

Emily tamped down on her feelings. "I realize this. It is concern for you that drives me to ask the question. If they suspect you, you may be in danger."

He carefully filled his pipe with tobacco. "The hierarchy is splintered," he said as he packed the bowl with his thumb. "Some disapprove of the new leadership, and it has led to suspicion and mistrust. Taking the hostages was not sanctioned by the supreme leader. She is angry with the captain and his officers, and they mistrust the rest of us enough to keep the information a secret in case one of us wanted to inform her."

Emily reeled from what he'd just said. It was more information than Mustafa had ever imparted at once, but Emily could only focus on one part: *she.* He'd said the supreme leader was a woman. Her heart began to pound. She was pretty sure this was information Ian and HOT didn't have. After the capture of Al Ahmad, the brotherhood had undergone a massive shake-up as the factions battled for control. Zaran had once been a candidate for the supreme leadership, and he'd wanted it pretty badly.

But the Freedom Force was much diminished from the days of Al Ahmad, and nothing happened fast. Zaran and a few other lieutenants had been locked in a battle for dominion. Zaran had been winning when she'd stabbed him with his own knife.

Emily's fingers shook as she reached for her water. There was finally a new leader if what Mustafa said was true. And she was a woman. It was nothing short of extraordinary.

And deeply, disturbingly frightening.

"Do you know who the supreme leader is?"

His eyes flashed as if he realized he'd revealed something he'd meant to keep secret. "No. She is called Raja. That is all."

Raja... Hope.

"If taking them was not sanctioned, why do they continue to hold them?"

His smile didn't reach his eyes. "There are some who believe the Americans might trade Al Ahmad for these people's lives."

Emily's throat went utterly dry. "That is unlikely. America doesn't negotiate with terrorists."

"And yet here you are."

It was said without irony.

"I'm here because my government wants to save them, yes. But if the Freedom Force makes this public, if they start to threaten the US directly, there will be no negotiation. Right now there's a chance—a chance for you to get all the money you desire to leave the organization and a chance to save the hostages with a minimum of bloodshed."

His dark eyes had sharpened. "How much money?"

Emily swallowed. She wasn't authorized to do this, but she had to take a chance. She was as tired of the game as he was. "One hundred thousand dollars."

Ian would burst a blood vessel, but if it got them the information, he could figure out how to explain the expense to his superiors later.

"Five hundred," Mustafa said coolly. "What you ask is risky."

Emily sat up straighter. Five hundred thousand? God, did they even have that much? Did she care? "I'll need proof. There'll be no payment without it."

"Two days," he said, standing. "You will come here with the money, and I will come with proof of the hostages' location."

"I can't come alone with that kind of cash."

He snorted. "As if you ever come alone, Light of Zaran. Yes, I know you have people watching us, and they will be watching us in two days as well." He leaned toward her. "If you do not deliver on your promise, you will have signed both our death warrants—because I will not go down alone."

TWELVE

EMILY WAITED FOR MUSTAFA TO LEAVE. She sat and sipped her water for a good fifteen minutes, her mind boiling with all she'd learned. Had she really just promised him half a million dollars for information?

She had, and Ian was going to kill her. But, dammit, the thought of Linda Cooper and her unborn child suffering at the hands of the Freedom Force was just too much to bear. Ian had an arsenal of expensive equipment, he never lacked for money or supplies, and for once he was working with the US government on this particular op.

So, yeah, he could get the money. He *had* to get the money.

But could Mustafa deliver? Was he merely jerking her around, or was he really going to find out where the hostages were being held?

Then again, maybe he'd known all along and he'd been waiting for just such a moment—her desperation to know where the hostages were. Had she played into his hands? Had she promised him the moon when she could have gotten away with less?

Emily took a deep breath and finished her water. Then she stood and wove her way between tables. Once outside, she started the long walk back to the compound. She scanned her surroundings, looking for anything out of place. There was nothing but people going about their daily tasks. Women with baskets of groceries, children playing in the dusty street, vendors with market stalls selling everything from vegetables to touristy gadgets. Not that Acamar had many tourists these days, but the excavation of the Lost City had brought hope they would have more—until the kidnapping.

It was always a shame when certain radical elements ruined opportunities for everyone. If the Freedom Force was spilling out into Acamar, that could be a sign they were regaining strength. It could also be a sign of discontent in the organization.

Speaking of which—a woman in charge? That was practically unheard of, or would have been just a few months ago. None of the women she'd known while she lived in Qu'rim had struck her as having even a remote chance of taking over the organization.

It was definitely a puzzle and one she couldn't wait to share with Ian and the HOT operatives. *This* was what being out here was all about. Making a difference. Being useful to her country.

Emily didn't see any sign of her bodyguard detachment, but she knew they were there, following along like the wake to her ship. Sweat rolled down the inside of her abaya and her heart pounded. She wanted to get back to the compound, but she had to stop for a minute. She walked in the shade of the buildings as much as possible, but the dust and heat were stifling nevertheless.

She pulled up and leaned back against a mud-brick building, wishing she could pull the abaya off and get more air. People passed her by without pause. Her mouth was as dry as the sand beneath her feet, and she wished she had more water.

Oddly enough, she also had to pee from all the water she'd drunk at the café. She stood there for several minutes, breathing evenly and cooling down, before she pushed away from the wall, determined to continue. The minute she was back at Ian's place, she could take this abaya off and stand in front of a fan with a bottle of cold water in her hand.

She just had to get that far. But her head swam and she stumbled as she felt suddenly light-headed. She reached out and caught herself on the hood of a car parked on the street.

Dammit. What the fuck was this?

Hands settled on her shoulders. She started to scream, but the hands turned her in time to see blue eyes staring back at her.

"Ryan, you have to let me go," she choked out. "Someone could see us."

"I don't give a fuck," he growled. "You're sick."

Before she could stop him, he swept her into his arms and strode down the street. She protested feebly, but he wasn't letting her go, so she tucked her head into his chest and clung to him. In truth, it felt nice to be moving down the street without having to do the work herself.

Soon they reached Ian's compound and Ryan passed into the interior courtyard. He still didn't put her down. Emily kicked her legs, though her stomach boiled when she did so.

"Put me down, Ry. We're here."

"Like fuck." He turned his head and barked at someone. "She needs medical attention. Now."

Emily clutched his tunic in her fists. "No, I'm fine. Just hot. Makes me light-headed."

This was not the triumphant return she'd been envisioning. But Ryan didn't stop, and he didn't put her down. He carried her up the stairs and then stopped in the darkened hallway.

"Which one's yours?"

"How do you know I have a room up here? I could be in one of the other buildings."

He snorted. "You're here. Now tell me which one before I start kicking in doors."

Emily steamed. "Second on the left."

Ryan strode over and opened the door, then he carried her inside and laid her on the bed. She promptly sprang upright, intending to shove him out the door, but her stomach rebelled and she went down again.

"Goddamn it, Emily, why are you fighting? You've got a virus or something, and you need to be still."

"I don't need you here to do it." She ripped at the abaya until he came over and caught the edge, lifting it up and over her head.

He dropped it on a chair and continued to loom over her. It was nothing like the night he'd loomed over her in his apartment, all sexy and naked and hard.

"I have to pee," she said, trying to shove the thought of a hard Ryan from her mind.

"Need help getting there?"

"No." She stood, more carefully this time, and made her way down the hall to the bathroom. She knew Ryan was standing in her open door and watching to make sure she didn't disappear in the other direction.

She would if she didn't have to pee—and if she didn't feel like hell.

When she opened the door again, he was still standing there watching her. She made her way slowly back to her room, then sat in the chair in front of the fan. There was air-conditioning, but she also kept a fan for when the AC just didn't get the job done.

Boots clomped on the stairs, and then Jared appeared in the door along with Ian.

"What happened?" Ian asked, and Ryan sneered at him.

"You sent her out there when she's sick. What do you think happened?"

Ian growled. "I wasn't talking to you, fuckwad."

Emily's heart thumped. Jared ripped open his medical kit and pulled out a blood pressure cuff.

"I got light-headed again. I'll be fine after I sit here for a bit. And I could use some water. Someone want to get it for me?"

Ryan didn't move. Neither did Ian. Jared looked up from where he had the cuff around her arm. He pressed the stethoscope to her veins and lifted an eyebrow.

"Well, I can't get it," he grumbled.

Ian swore before whirling and disappearing down the stairs. Then he was back with two bottles of water. Emily took one and twisted off the cap before drinking gratefully. God, that felt good.

"Pressure's up," Jared said, "but that's not surprising. Tell me what's been going on, Emily. Don't leave any-thing out."

Emily glared at Ryan and Ian. "I don't need an audience for this."

Jared turned to look at them both. "True. Why don't you two give us some privacy?"

Ryan's jaw tightened. Ian shrugged.

"I'll go," Ryan said, "but I'll be right outside."

"It's none of your business, Ryan. Just go away."

He looked militant. "Not happening, sweetheart." Then he stalked out of the room, and she knew he'd taken up residence in the hall.

Ian started to follow Ryan. "Let me know what's up, Jared."

He left the room and closed the door behind him. Emily let out the breath she'd been holding.

"Wow," Jared said.

"Yeah, wow."

"Anytime you're ready."

She began to recite her symptoms while Jared listened. He nodded and frowned a bit. When she finished, he only stared at her.

"Emily, when was your last period?"

Her cheeks flamed. "I can't be pregnant," she hissed. "It's impossible."

"Doesn't sound impossible. Have you had sex in the past three months?"

"Yes." She shook her head. "But I've been tested. When I was married. The doctor said I'd never get pregnant."

"Doctors aren't perfect. I think, before we go any further, you need to take a pregnancy test. We can eliminate it as a cause."

Eliminate it as a cause. She didn't know why those

words made her panic, but they did. "I'm just hot. And tired."

Jared's expression was patient. "That may be, but your symptoms are consistent with the first trimester of pregnancy."

She appreciated that he kept his voice low, but frustration hammered at her. She shoved her hand through her hair. Her scalp was still damp, but she was feeling much better now that she had water and a fan.

Emily lowered her head and stared at her lap for a long moment. She couldn't deny that a tiny part of her wanted to believe it was possible. But submitting to a pregnancy test, getting her hopes up—though being terrified too because she wasn't really ready for a baby in her life—and then being let down when the doctor's diagnosis was confirmed? Soul crushing.

She'd been there before, so to go through it again? To be told, again, she couldn't do the most basic thing a woman's body was designed to do? It was almost too much. But yes, she had to do it. If there was even the slightest chance, she needed to know. No matter how painful it was to submit to something that would call up all her old feelings of failure and inadequacy.

"Fine. Let's get this over with."

Jared reached into his bag for a cup. "If you can get me some urine, I'll test it for HCG."

Emily snatched the cup and stood. She'd just gone, but she'd drunk enough water that she could definitely go again.

"Sorry, Em," Jared said.

"It's okay. Best to get it out of the way and find out what's really wrong, right?"

THIRTEEN

EMILY WAS TIGHT-LIPPED WHEN she emerged from her room. Ryan searched her face but there was no hint of what was going on in her expression. She clutched a lidded plastic cup in her hand as she sailed down the hallway to the bathroom.

A pee test?

Ryan went to stand in the door to her room. Jared the former PJ gave him a nod.

"Any ideas?" Ryan asked.

"A couple."

"And?"

Jared sighed. "You don't really think I'm telling you, right? That's up to her."

Ryan turned to look at the closed bathroom door. Emily was inside there, presumably peeing in a cup. He wasn't sure why that was necessary, but he wasn't a medic—or not this kind of medic. All Special Operators were trained in combat medicine, but Jared was more than that. And he wasn't telling Ryan anything.

A few minutes later, Emily appeared again. She

walked past him as if he weren't there and then shut her bedroom door in his face. He resisted the urge to break the door in, but only barely. When the door opened again, the PJ walked out first. Emily was right behind him, still with her nose in the air, still ignoring Ryan.

He caught up to her as she headed down the stairs and put a hand on her shoulder. She stopped and whirled to face him.

"Don't touch me. You have no right to touch me."

No, he didn't.

But, goddammit, he wanted to. And not like this. He wanted more, but he dropped his hand to his side and clenched it into a fist.

"What did he say?"

She couldn't hold his gaze. "It's none of your business, Ryan. I'll be fine."

He hated that she wouldn't tell him. He hated the mistrust and hostility that characterized their interactions now. It was such a far cry from how they'd been just two months ago. She'd been a friend. She'd told him everything, and now she told him nothing. It hurt, oddly enough.

"I didn't stop caring what happened to you just because you ran away, Emily."

Her eyes softened a fraction. Then she started down the stairs again. "I have a job to do, Ry. You want to stop me, and I can't let that happen."

She halted at the bottom and turned to face him. Her eyes were pleading this time. "If you care about me, then you have to let me do this. You have to stand back and stop interfering."

Fuck, he felt like she was maneuvering him into a corner. He did care. A lot. He swallowed. "I'm not interfering. I'm trying to protect you."

She snorted. "Your idea of protecting me is tossing me on a plane and sending me back to the States."

He couldn't deny it. "Yeah, well, you'd be safer that way."

"So would you, and yet here you are. Willing to risk your life to save people you've never met."

"It's my job."

"And this is mine. I have to go talk to Ian about the meeting with Mustafa."

He hated the way she said Black's name. Hated that she was so comfortable with Black, and that she wasn't with him anymore. Jealousy pricked him hard.

"Are you and Black a thing now?" he asked.

She gaped at him for a second. And then her face turned red. "What? No! Dammit, Ryan, why would you ask that? Because he's a man? Because I can't function on my own without a man to hold my hand? Jesus, what is it with you?"

She stormed off toward Black's office with Ryan on her heels. "I have a right to know, Emily. I asked because you left my bed and went with him."

She whirled on him again. At this rate, they'd reach Black's office sometime around midnight.

"I went with him because he promised to clear my name. I explained that already. Yes, I wanted to fix my life and make you and Victoria proud—but now I know that I'm needed here, and I want to help get these hostages free. I want to put all the knowledge I have of the Freedom Force to use and stop them before they hurt more people. Don't you think I have that right? That *duty?*"

He hated that she made sense. That she was passionate about the things she was saying. Because he didn't want her here. He didn't want her anywhere near a war zone, and he didn't want her associating with the same people who'd caused her so much fear and pain. It was dangerous for her to meet with a member of the Freedom Force even if the man was selling information for his own profit. What if he decided there was more to be made by selling her out instead?

"You aren't trained for this kind of life."

"Fuck you. Yes, I am. *Life* trained me to be here. But Zaran trained me to shoot, and Ian's men trained me in hand-to-hand combat. I'm not you, but I can hold my own."

He rolled his neck to pop out the kinks. She frustrated him almost beyond endurance. If he picked her up, flung her over his shoulder, and hauled her back to her room where he could tie her to the bed and leave her, he still wouldn't be satisfied that she'd stay out of trouble.

She glared at him another second and then she started toward Black's office again. Black looked up when she entered with Ryan on her heels. He sat back at his desk and folded his hands over his stomach. He flicked a glance at Ryan before settling his gaze on Emily.

"Everything okay?"

"Jared is doing some tests. We'll know something later today."

"What kind of tests?"

"Tests," Emily ground out.

Ian shrugged. "All right. So what's up? How'd the meeting with Mustafa go?"

Emily glanced over her shoulder at Ryan.

"HOT needs to hear it one way or the other," Black

said. "Proceed."

Emily sank onto a chair and pushed the hair that had sprung free from her ponytail back over her ear. "I've learned there's a new supreme leader… and she's a woman."

Ryan's eyebrows climbed to his hairline. Black looked suitably stunned as well.

"Did you say a woman?"

"Yep, a woman. Her code name is Raja."

Black wrote this down. "We'll have to start listening for it."

Ryan couldn't help but be impressed that she'd learned this information. That didn't change his mind about wanting her to leave the Middle East, however.

Emily started sliding her thumb up and down her thigh. Fidgeting. "He's going to bring me the information on the hostages in two days' time."

"That's excellent," Black said.

Ryan didn't say a word. He could tell by the way she was acting that there was something more going on.

Finally she shook her head and met Black's gaze. "We'll need five hundred thousand in cash, Ian. It's the only way."

Black didn't look pleased. In fact, he looked a little nauseated, which amused Ryan to no end.

"Jesus, Emily. You should have cleared that with me first."

Emily thrust her chin out. "Yeah, well, I didn't have time. They're moving the hostages soon, so time's running out. They're taking them to Qu'rim, to a remote camp in the desert—I thought you'd prefer we didn't go back to square one."

"I'd prefer we didn't give half a million to a fucking terrorist."

"I'd prefer it too—but that's his price. What do you want to do? Say no way? The Freedom Force's price is going to be much higher when they get around to mentioning it…"

She let the sentence trail off. Black's gaze sharpened. "Which is?"

"They want Al Ahmad."

Holy shit. But there was no way the US was ever letting Al Ahmad free from Guantanamo. They all knew it too.

Black raked a hand through his hair. "Fuck."

"Exactly," Emily said.

There was a knock on the wall and the three of them swung around to see Jared in the open door. "Got a second, Emily?"

Ian unlocked the secure server room and went inside to make a phone call from the secure sat phone. He had one on his desk, but this one was more private. He dialed the special number in Washington and waited for his handler to pick up.

"Hello, Odysseus," his handler said, using his code name. "Is all well on your ship?"

Ian snorted. "I've got two HOT squads under my roof, a girl who's more trouble than I thought she'd be, and the usual assortment of troubles from any number of quarters. Sure, everything's absolutely fine."

Phoenix laughed. "Sounds like fun. I sometimes miss fieldwork."

"Come on over. We'll find you a bed."

"Mmm, hardly. What have you got for me? You wouldn't be calling if it wasn't good."

"Emily's learned that the Freedom Force has a new leader. A woman called Raja."

Phoenix whistled. "Wow, now that's something worth knowing. Any idea who this Raja is?"

He'd been thinking about it for a while. He'd had contact with the Freedom Force over the past couple of years, selling them things, doing dirty deeds for them—though never anything too dirty—and basically proving he was a man with no morals so they'd trust him with their business.

"I wish I knew. There weren't really any women in the hierarchy, not typically. Behind the scenes, sure. Wives of powerful men. But no active lieutenants."

"Could it be a wife? What about Al Ahmad's wife?"

"Fatima al-Faizan? I doubt it. She was decorative, not a part of the organization at all. She seemed stunned when the truth came out."

Phoenix sighed. "Maybe a woman who joined the cause and worked her way up through the ranks quite suddenly. There was a power vacuum when Zaran bin Yusuf was killed that might have enabled someone to take advantage."

"Maybe."

"Does Emily have any ideas? She was a part of the organization for three years."

111

"I haven't asked her yet. There was a HOT operator in the room at the time."

"I see. I suppose Mendez is hearing the same news right about now."

"Yes, I imagine he is." And wondering the same things about who Raja might be.

"This is tricky, Odysseus. I didn't want HOT there, but I was overruled. Cooperating with them is dangerous to our overall mission, like talking to me is dangerous for you, so the faster we get those hostages free, the sooner you can go back to business as usual."

He knew Phoenix was right. Sometimes he hated business as usual. But smoking out traitors in the belly of your own government was a worthy cause—and one that could get him killed if he didn't tread carefully. He'd alienated himself from the good guys and made himself into one of the bad guys—or at least one of the guys who didn't care where his money came from so long as it kept on coming. It had taken years and a lot of sacrifice—and he couldn't go back now.

Officially, he was disavowed. Unofficially, he was deep black. Ironic, considering his name. Sometimes he missed Langley. Sometimes he missed *normal*.

"There's something else," Ian said, knowing Phoenix wasn't going to be pleased about the money. He kept a million in cash for bribes, equipment, etc. Losing half of that in a chunk was going to hurt. "We may know where the hostages are in two days' time… but it comes with a price."

"How much of a price?"

"Half a million."

Phoenix swore. "Do you trust the asset to deliver?"

Ian fixed his gaze on the stone wall outside the Faraday cage. "Not particularly, no."

"Then I assume you have a backup plan?"

"Yes."

"Good."

Phoenix didn't ask what the plan was, and Ian didn't say. He knew his handler didn't want the details. Phoenix wanted results.

FOURTEEN

PREGNANT.

Emily clutched the piece of paper in her hand that reported her HCG levels were consistent with pregnancy. Jared couldn't date the pregnancy, but Emily knew. There was only one possibility.

One illicit night with Ryan two months ago and she was pregnant. Her eyes filled with tears as fury rolled in her belly.

Not fury that she was pregnant, but fury at Zaran, at the doctor who'd told her she would never have children. She'd believed she was damaged, incapable. Not complete, even though she knew the ability to have children didn't define her as a woman.

"You'll need to get checked. An ultrasound, prenatal appointments. I'll give you something to help the nausea, but you'll have to be careful in this heat. Stay indoors during midday, hydrate, get plenty of rest."

She looked up at Jared through blurry eyes. She'd followed him from Ian's office until they'd found a private corner to speak in. The news he'd given her had stolen her breath. And her voice, it seemed.

All she could do was nod.

Jared put a hand on her shoulder and squeezed. "It'll be all right, Em. You'll figure it out."

Would she? They both knew this would be the end of her work here. She nodded again. Jared dropped his hand back to his side.

"I can arrange a visit to a women's clinic. There are a few good ones here in Al-Izir. You can at least get started while you figure out what to do next."

Somehow, she found her voice. "Next week."

"Sure."

Because she needed to meet with Mustafa in two days, and she needed to take half a million dollars with her. Part of her wanted to fold up shop and get on the next plane home, but she couldn't do it. Now, more than ever, she had to do this job and clear her name. She had to do it for her baby, or the poor thing would *never* have a normal life.

Neither would she. And neither would her baby's father.

A chill slid through her. Ryan. Oh God, how could she tell him? What would he say? She knew, without a doubt, that he'd redouble his insistence that she leave Acamar. She clenched the paper in her hand and gritted her teeth.

That was *not* happening. Not yet. She had to help find those hostages, and she had to hope that was enough for Ian to live up to his promise.

Jared handed her a bottle of nausea medication from his kit and explained how to take it. Then he left her there to gather her wits. Emily sucked in a breath before swiping at her eyes and sniffling. She took the stairs up to her room.

But when she opened the door, the room was occupied. Ryan stood at the window, looking somehow bigger and more imposing than he'd been earlier. He turned as she entered. Fury churned inside her belly, but there was also a healthy dose of fear this time.

"So now you trespass whenever you please? Nice."

She closed the door behind her and shoved the paper and bottle Jared had given her into her pants pocket. Not that they were hidden considering the bulge or the fact Ryan had seen her put them there. Her heart beat harder.

"Figured this was the one place you couldn't avoid me."

"What do you want?"

He nodded at the bulge on her hip. "What did Jared say?"

Oh fucking hell. Her heart skipped a beat and sweat broke out on her torso. She had to tell him. But how could she tell him right now, right here?

Ryan, you're going to be a father.

The thought made her stomach lurch.

"Rest, hydrate, stay inside midday. I'll be fine."

Ryan didn't look convinced. "That's it? After the fainting and throwing up? After all I've seen you eat is bread, and not a lot of it?"

Heat marched across her skin. "You've been here barely twenty-four hours, and my stomach was upset. I expect I'll eat more today."

And she would once she got the antinausea meds into her system.

"What aren't you telling me, Emily?"

She reached around to twist her ponytail into a bun, securing it with a couple of pins sitting on her bedside table. Then she put her hands on her hips and stared at him. "I'm telling you what you need to know. There's nothing more."

Liar.

He stalked toward her, his big form imposing on her space. When he stopped in front of her, she was afraid to take a step back. Afraid that doing so would reveal too much. He loomed over her, his blue eyes searching hers.

And then he reached out with one hand and skimmed his fingers beneath her jaw, forcing her to tilt her head up to meet his gaze evenly when she'd dropped her lashes over her eyes.

"You forget that I know you, Emily." His voice was soft, gravelly, and she wanted to sink into it. Into him.

Her heart thudded and her skin burned—and she was positive he could see her pulse throbbing in her throat. Giving herself away.

"You don't know me that well," she croaked.

His mouth twisted ironically. "No, you're right about that. Had no idea you'd come to me that night to give me a good-bye fuck. Couldn't have predicted that one." He leaned toward her, his eyes searching, always searching. "But I've learned to tell when you're hiding something, thanks to that night. And you definitely are."

He took another step closer until he was fully in her space. She felt as if she were paralyzed. She couldn't move a muscle. And then his hand was on her hip, his fingers sliding downward—

Into her pocket.

"No," she cried as he pulled the bottle and paper free.

She snatched at it, but he held it up high, out of her reach. "You have no right!"

"I have no right? I spent months listening to you whenever you needed an ear, talking to you when you wanted to talk, being your friend. I did that at a cost to myself, Emily. I hid it from everyone, from my superiors, from your sister. I did it because you needed someone. I was there for you when you said you were afraid, and I was there for you when you wanted to perform a fucking experiment with my body. You wanted it even though I told you that was the one line I couldn't cross. The one thing I wasn't supposed to do. So what did I do when you insisted? I fucking gave in, because you asked it. Because you said you needed me. And what did you do? You left. You disappeared without any explanation, back into a life that you knew none of us would approve of. You took advantage of me, of the team, of your sister. And now you say I don't have a right to know what's wrong with you?"

Emily trembled from head to toe. She'd screwed this up so badly. Screwed up everything. She'd been trying to do the right thing, to fix her life, but she'd ended up hurting the people she loved the most instead. And she hated feeling guilty about that, especially when she *knew* she was doing good work. That her meetings with Mustafa were making a difference.

"Ryan," she choked out.

His expression was granite. "Tell me what's on this paper, Emily." He held it without opening it. Held the bottle without reading it. His eyes bored into hers. "If you ever cared about me, if anything you ever said was real, then tell me what's on this paper."

"If I don't want to?"

"Then I'll walk out of here and never ask you another thing. We'll be finished for good."

Emily swallowed. "I thought we were finished already. I thought you hated me for leaving."

"I don't hate you. I'm pissed, but I don't hate you. Lie to me about this, and that just might change."

She put her hands over her face and took deep breaths. My God, she'd barely processed this news at all, and now he was demanding to know what was wrong. She wanted to laugh and cry at the same time. Being pregnant with the child of the man you loved was supposed to be joyous.

Yet there was no joy here. And there would be none when she told him. He wasn't going to be happy about it. He wasn't going to ask her to marry him.

She didn't expect to feel his arms around her suddenly, but that's what happened. Didn't expect to be dragged against his big body and held close. She couldn't help but clutch her hands into his shirt and press her face to his chest. He smelled good. Like sun and sand and Ryan.

She dragged in a breath that came out as a sob even though she tried to stop it.

He squeezed her tight. "There's nothing you can't tell me, honey. Whatever it is, I'll help you through it. We'll get you to a doctor, get you taken care of. You don't have to suffer."

Emily couldn't help but laugh, though it was a broken sound that was as much sob as humor. "Oh, Ryan, it's nothing like that. I'm not dying."

She sniffed and pushed back until she could look him in the eye. His brows were drawn low as he studied her. Her heart hammered and she felt light-headed again.

She dropped her gaze to her fists clutching his shirt. "I'm not dying," she repeated.

"Then what?"

She didn't want to say it. But she had to. "That doctor was wrong. The one in Qu'rim. He said I… I couldn't g-get p-pregnant."

Ryan's body tightened like a steel coil. He pushed her back a step, his hands on her shoulders, the bottle and paper falling forgotten to the floor. There was confusion in that gaze. And pain.

"Are you telling me you're pregnant? Right now?"

She nodded.

"Jesus." He stepped back and raked a hand through his hair. It was longer than military regs allowed, but in HOT the regs didn't apply when the object was to blend into their surroundings. "You're pregnant… I didn't think…" His nostrils flared. "Whose is it?"

Emily went still. Had he really just asked…? Heat and ice flashed over her skin in rapid succession. And then the anger began to build. The injustice of it. And, worse, the suspicion that if he could think she'd been with someone else since their night together, he most certainly had.

She whirled, clenching her hands at her sides before she launched herself at him and wrapped them around his throat. Closed her eyes and sucked in breath after breath to keep from imploding right here and now.

"You can ask me that?" she grated. "After that night? When you know why I came to you? Why it had to be you?"

Silence…

"Wait a minute. Are you telling me…?"

She whirled around again, pretty sure she wouldn't

wrap her hands around his neck now. "Yes," she yelled. "That's exactly what I'm telling you, you prick! This baby is *yours!*"

FIFTEEN

"DUDE, YOU OKAY?"

Ryan looked up from where he'd been leaning back in his chair, two of its legs off the floor, listening to his guys talk about the mission. Fiddler was looking at him strangely. No, fuck, they all were.

"Yeah, fine. Why?"

"You seem a million miles away."

Brandy caught his gaze, looked away. Brandy hadn't been there yesterday for the revelation that Emily had been in Ryan's bed the night before she'd disappeared, but the man knew something was up. Knew and had probably already told Victoria. Yeah, Ryan's balls were definitely in danger now.

Not that he fucking cared. He had bigger things to worry about.

Emily was pregnant. With his kid. What. The. Fuck.

"It's been nonstop since we left DC. I'm fucking tired."

Which was bullshit because Special Operators were accustomed to going without sleep, without showers, without food except stuff that was dried and tasted like tree bark for days at a time. Hell, the number of times he'd brewed coffee in a fucking tin cup with a Sterno can and stale water. It tasted like day-old socks, but it provided the caffeine jolt a military operative needed.

"You can go to bed as soon as we're done here, princess."

"Fuck you, Ice," Ryan said.

"All right, assholes," Matt said. "It's been a long day. Let's wrap this up and get some R & R while we can."

"So it's two more days," Kev "Big Mac" MacDonald said, "and we'll hopefully know where the hostages are being held. Unless something shakes out sooner."

"Could be a double cross," Cade Rodgers said. The Echo squad leader didn't say much, but when he did it was usually memorable. And not in the best way.

"Could be," Matt replied. "We won't know until Emily meets with Mustafa again."

Ryan's gut churned. *Meets with Mustafa again?* Over his dead fucking body.

Brandy's nostrils flared as he sat up straight. "Ain't nobody sending my almost-sister-in-law into a goddamn double cross situation. Victoria will gut me if anyone touches a hair on Emily's head."

"Don't see as we have a choice," Big Mac said. "She works for Black. She's the contact."

Matt held up a hand to quiet them. "Look, we haven't given up on our intel finding the location first. We have analysts working day and night back at HQ."

"If Emily goes, I'm going with her," Brandy said.

Ryan's chair hit the floor with a thump that reverberated through the room. "Me too."

Everyone looked at him. No one said anything.

"We'll figure out who's going where when the time comes," Matt growled. "That's not up for discussion yet."

Brandy looked militant.

Ryan stood. He couldn't sit here another second. Not when his skin felt like it was stretched too tight and about to split apart at any moment. His emotions churned like a hurricane. He had to get out of here, get some air. "We done here?"

Fiddler's brows rose. Cade Rodgers looked at him as if he were watching a bitch fight about to happen and enjoying it immensely. Ice openly gaped, which would have been funny if Ryan were in the mood for funny.

Matt's brows drew together. Then he nodded as if he'd decided something. "Yeah, you're done, Flash. For now."

Ryan strode out of the room, his eyes burning, his gut churning, his breath razoring in and out of his lungs. It wasn't late, but it was dark now. He hadn't seen Emily in hours, not since she'd told him she was pregnant and he'd felt like she'd hammered a fist right into the center of his belly.

He'd stupidly forgotten who he was dealing with as his mind had churned over her words. Asking her whose baby it was had been automatic. And the minute he'd done so, he'd known it was the wrong question. He could still see the hurt on her face, the defeat in the set of her shoulders as she'd turned away.

He'd known he was the only one. Known he'd spent an entire night making love to her without any protection whatsoever. Because she'd told him she couldn't get pregnant.

He'd believed it. Hell, *she'd* believed it. Or had she? What if it had been a trick?

He hated that he thought that, but goddamn it, she'd proved he didn't know her as well as he'd thought he did when she ran away. Those were the thoughts whirling through his mind when she'd told him the baby was his.

"Say something," she'd said.

He hadn't been capable of saying anything for several minutes. Hell, even now he couldn't remember what he'd finally said when he could speak. What they'd talked about. It hadn't lasted long, and then he'd found himself outside her door, staring at it. She'd closed it in his face.

He crossed the compound, nodding at the man who guarded the wall. The man nodded back, then spit into the dirt as he continued his circuit. Ryan was bunking with Fiddler in a small room at the opposite end of the compound, but that's not where he was headed. He passed inside the main house and toward the stairs leading to the second floor. Ian Black stepped out of his office, lifted an eyebrow. But he didn't stop Ryan as he went up the stairs.

He came to a halt outside her door, his heart thrumming, his brain burning. He hadn't said the right things earlier. Hell, he didn't know what the right things were. He lifted his fist and pounded on the door.

A second later, it opened. Emily stood there in a T-shirt and camouflage pants, her hair flowing loose and free, her dark eyes full of hurt and suspicion. Dear God, this woman was having *his* baby.

Of all the things he'd ever considered doing, kids were a distant—seriously distant—thought. His lifestyle wasn't conducive to a kid, though his brain reminded him that Ice had a kid and handled it all right, especially now that he had Grace in his life.

Yet Ryan had been raised right, and he knew what he was supposed to do. His father had married his mother, in spite of her nuttiness, and he'd been there for Ryan when his mother finally fell apart. His father had always been a rock. A calm, guiding spirit who didn't lay blame or shove off responsibilities.

Ryan could do no less. His father would be ashamed if he did.

The words tumbled out. "We need to get married."

Emily's eyebrows climbed her forehead. Then they arrowed down again and her face reddened.

"That's just about the sweetest proposal ever, Ry— but no."

She pushed the door closed. Ryan stuck his foot between the jamb and the door before she could shut it all the way. She ripped it back open and glared at him.

"What?"

He blinked. His heart was an organ completely out of his control right now. It pounded, his head throbbing in time with the blood pulsing through his body. "What do you mean what? You're pregnant. I'm here to do the right thing."

She crossed her arms and cocked a hip. "Oh really? It only took you..." She glanced down at the Fitbit she wore and pressed the button for the watch function. "Six hours. Six hours since I told you I was pregnant to decide that you want to marry me? No thanks."

He threw his arms wide. "What do you want me to say? You shocked me. I had to think."

She snorted. "Dude. If you had to think that hard about asking me to marry you, then no, it's not the right thing for you to do."

Goddammit. She was driving him crazy here. Fucking insane. What the hell did she want from him anyway?

"You're pregnant."

"I know that, genius."

Ryan closed his eyes for a second. "Can we just talk for ten fucking minutes without all the hostility?"

She stepped away from the door and went to sit in the only chair in the room. Ryan closed the bedroom door behind him and watched her as she folded her arms over her breasts and crossed her legs. The message was certainly clear—she was shutting him out.

He let his gaze slide over the room. It was bare of any furniture but a twin bed, a chair with a small desk, and a dresser. But she'd managed to make it cozy for herself. There was a woven tribal rug on the floor, a sheet that hung over the single window, a few books on the desk, and a lamp that she'd put a sheer piece of fabric over. The fabric had come from one of the markets, he'd bet, its edges dripping with metallic coin-like objects that would rattle when shaken.

"What do you want to say?" She regarded him like a queen surveying her subject. Haughty. Proud.

He didn't like it. "I think there's a lot to say, don't you? We're having a baby together, and that changes everything."

"It does. But I'm not marrying you because you believe it's something you *have* to do. I know what it's like when your partner starts to resent you for being unable to have a baby. I'd rather not find out what it's like to have one who resents me because I had a baby instead."

"I'm not going to resent you."

"How do you know that, Ryan?" She clasped a hand over her still-flat belly. "How do you know you won't hate being a parent? Won't hate that you have to change diapers or put up with tantrums or get up at two a.m.? And what about when you have to consider two other people in your decision making because it's not just you anymore?"

Ryan blinked. "You're having twins?"

Emily growled. "No, I'm not having twins. I meant me! You have to consider me and what I want too."

Jesus, he was an idiot. "Yeah, I get that." He shoved a hand through his hair. "This is a lot to process."

"It is for me too."

He went over and knelt beside Emily's chair. Then he reached out and swept his fingers along her soft cheek. She didn't flinch, didn't pull away, and he found that encouraging. There was something rather frightening about the idea of her refusing his proposal, as if she were shutting him out of her life.

"Marry me, Emily. We'll figure it out. We'll make it work. I'm not bin Yusuf. I'll take care of you."

SIXTEEN

EMILY TREMBLED AS A SHIVER skated over her body. Ryan was touching her. Gently, sweetly, in a way that he hadn't touched her since that night in his apartment. It was so tempting. So damn tempting to say yes.

Her heart begged her to say yes. If she married him, she could make him love her.

No. That was exactly the kind of thinking that had led her into a downward spiral when she'd been a teen. You didn't *make* people love you. Thinking you could only led to heartbreak.

"I can't," she whispered, dropping her head until her hair fell forward and curtained her face from his view. There were so many reasons. He didn't love her. He would end up resenting her no matter what he said. And marrying her meant the end of his career unless she finished this mission and Ian kept his promise.

Maybe it *still* meant an end of his career, even with her name cleared. Because HOT would know who she was and Colonel Mendez would be furious that Ryan had been involved with her in the first place.

"Do you honestly want to do this alone?"

She lifted her head to meet his gaze. His blue eyes glittered like hot flames.

"No… but that doesn't mean we have to marry."

"I'm trying to do right by you. What the hell do you think Brandy will do to me once he finds out? Or, worse, your sister?"

Emily's belly churned with irritation. "Do you think I care what they think right now? Victoria is half a world away—and Nick's your teammate. He's not a fool, and he's not going to suggest pistols at dawn or anything. He only worries about me insomuch as my welfare affects Victoria's."

How could she tell him that she would have married him in a second if he'd asked for any other reason than it was his duty because he'd knocked her up? How could she admit to what she felt for him when it was abundantly clear he didn't feel the same way?

He'd only ever felt sorry for her and responsible in some way, even before the baby. She didn't doubt that he cared, in his own fashion, but she knew he didn't love her. And dammit, that's what she wanted out of life now. She was old enough and had been through enough to know what she wanted.

She wanted a man who loved her, who couldn't live without her because doing so would leave him incomplete. She wanted passion and equality—in short, she wanted what Victoria had with Nick. That man worshipped her. Worshipped the ground she walked on. He'd do anything for her, sacrifice anything for her happiness.

Emily might not have known what real love between a couple was if she hadn't watched her sister and Nick over the past few months.

Now that she knew, she didn't want to settle for less in her own life. Maybe she was deluding herself, but she had to believe there was more for her too.

"I don't know how else to fix this, Emily. Marrying is the right thing to do for our kid. You'll be my dependent, eligible for medical care and my life insurance if something happens to me. We'd get housing and benefits from the military. You could go back to school, finish your degree. You wouldn't have to worry about finding a job or a place to live."

Yes, she knew all those things were important. But it was so cut-and-dried, so raw and logical. Not an ounce of feeling in there. Not an ounce of passion. Just practicality. And he still hadn't even addressed the biggest question of all, which was his job in HOT. He had to know what he was risking, but he acted like it didn't exist.

"Once more, you are *alllll* romance, big guy." She pushed away and stood. He looked up from his kneeling position, and her heart skipped a beat at the perfection of that face. "The answer is still no."

He got to his feet, scowling hard. "You aren't thinking this through, Emily."

"I'm thinking just fine. I don't want to get married because it'll make you feel better. I want to get married because you can't imagine life without me."

He didn't say anything, and she died just a little inside.

"Life isn't a romance novel," he said, eyes flashing.

Emily snorted. "Seriously? Who are you telling? I'm the poster child for dysfunctional relationships—which is why I'm not going to marry you like this." She shook her head. "I wish it were different, Ry. I wish we were in love, dating, and you wanted to marry me because you just had to spend your life with me. Because you *knew* deep in your heart and soul that I was the only person for you. But that's not what's happening here, and we both know it. So please stop trying to bully me into marriage for the sake of your conscience."

He clenched his fists at his sides. "You aren't shutting me out of this kid's life, Emily."

"I didn't say I was!"

His brows arrowed downward. Then he pointed at her. "Let me tell you something else while we're at it. You aren't endangering my kid's life, or yours, by continuing to work for Ian Black. I want you on the next plane out of here. I want you safe."

And there it was. His real motive for coming here. "I'm not going. If I leave now, those hostages are dead. Do you really want that to happen? Linda Cooper is pregnant, her husband's waiting for her at Aviano Air Base, probably praying to God that she comes home safely with their child—and you want me to get on a plane when I'm on the verge of getting the location out of my contact? No. Fucking. Way."

"You don't have to be here. Hassan Mustafa wants the money, and he doesn't care who delivers it. You're leaving."

Emily folded her arms over her chest. "I'm really not. I'll go when this is over, but not a moment sooner."

He didn't look any happier, but he tilted his head and considered her. "You'll go willingly when the hostages are free? Back to DC and the life you had before?"

The life she had before. He made it sound like it was

this awesome thing, when in fact she'd been lost and lonely and, well, purposeless in so many ways.

"Yes, Ryan, I'll go back. I don't have much choice. I'm not having my baby in Acamar. I'm not very useful to Ian if I can't go into the field anymore—and I can't with a child, can I?" She pulled a deep breath. "I'll go back and finish my degree, go to work and make a life for me and the baby. I promise you that."

"You still aren't meeting with Mustafa. One of us can go."

Her blood boiled over. She'd never realized just how autocratic he was. He'd never told her what to do before—not ever—but since he'd arrived yesterday, he hadn't stopped bossing her around for a single minute.

"You don't get to decide that."

"I'm not letting you go, Emily."

"You don't have a choice. I work for Ian, not you. I'm going."

"Do you even give a shit about this baby? About yourself?"

Emily launched herself at him, prepared to slap him upside his arrogant head, but he caught her raised arm and held her tight. She brought the other one up, but he caught that arm too.

"You're an asshole! Let go!"

He didn't hold her too tightly, but his grip was firm, his fingers pressing into her wrists, immobilizing her. Then he pushed her arms down, behind her back, and caught both wrists in one hand before slamming her full length against him.

Emily gasped at the sudden pressure of his body against hers. His heat seared into her, reminded her forcefully of that night they'd spent together when the heat between them had been incendiary.

Ryan was all muscle. All brawn and hard-bodied yumminess. And her core melted at the contact. It infuriated her and alarmed her too. How could she be firm with him when all he had to do was touch her like this and her entire body dissolved into a puddle of warm, syrupy desire?

If he asked her to marry him now, she'd probably agree. In fact, she'd probably agree to anything if it meant she could feel more of his body against hers—and she hated herself for it. He was her weakness, her addiction.

And it was worse because she didn't affect him the same way, didn't matter to him at all—

His cock swelled, the pressure against her belly growing. She tilted her head back, her mouth dropping open slightly. His gaze was fierce, possessive.

Vaguely, she knew she was supposed to be fighting him, insisting that he let her go—but she couldn't think of a thing to say when he looked at her like that, when his body pressed into hers and his cock grew hard.

He speared his free hand into her hair, tilted her head back. "Emily. Jesus, what you do to me…"

"What, Ry?" she whispered, her throat tight and raw. "What do I do to you?"

"This," he growled—and then he kissed her.

SEVENTEEN

HE WAS FURIOUS AND FRUSTRATED all at once. Ryan wanted to lock Emily in her room and not let her out until he could put her on a plane to the States, but she was too stubborn, too determined to do what she wanted.

He hadn't meant to kiss her. Hadn't meant to let her know that she had his brain twisted into knots and his libido revving into overdrive.

But goddamn, she was sexy. And sweet, so damn sweet.

Her lips softened beneath his, and he groaned as his tongue slid into her mouth. She was like honey and silk, her tongue meeting his softly, then a little harder as he tipped her head back for better access.

He let her wrists free, half certain she'd shove him away.

She did not. Her arms went up, around his neck, and she arched her body into his. Her sweet, perfect little body that nestled his child inside.

Oh, God.

It was such a staggering thought. An overwhelming

feeling. It had the power to bring him to his knees if he thought about it too much.

Emily Royal was pregnant with his baby. And she wouldn't let him protect her. Wouldn't let him do what was second nature to him, which was keep her and their child safe from harm.

He'd take a bullet for her. For them. She didn't understand.

She wanted him to marry her because he couldn't live without her. He was pretty sure he could live without anyone. His childhood had taught him that. He'd learned to live without a mother, and he'd survived it. Hell, he'd thrived after he'd finally come to accept what she was and that she was no good for his life.

So, yeah, he *could* live without anyone. But wanting to—that was another matter.

He slid his hands down Emily's sides, gently worked her shirt free from her pants. Then his palms skimmed up her bare skin, feeling the heat and silkiness of her. She shuddered beneath his touch, and his cock strained against his fly, aching to be let free. To be touched.

He hadn't been with a woman since he'd been with her. Hell, he hadn't been with any woman for about six months before he'd slept with Emily, truth be told—and he was primed. Fucking primed to go off like a rocket.

His fingers touched the lacy softness of her bra, and then he rounded her breasts and cupped them. She gasped as he glided his thumbs over her hardened nipples. He pressed a little harder, a little rougher, and she moaned.

Had she been this sensitive before? He didn't think she had, but maybe pregnancy made a difference.

Shit. She was pregnant and he had to be careful with

her. He'd never been with a pregnant woman, but he knew they were more delicate.

He left her breasts and smoothed his way down to her ass, which he cupped as he pulled her against his body, increasing the pressure in his groin.

He wanted to rip her clothes off and bury himself inside her, but he sensed that wasn't necessarily the way to go here. Because once it was over, there would be recriminations. Regrets and pain. He didn't want to cause her more pain.

He didn't want to cause himself more pain. *This*—this being with her and knowing she carried his child, this infuriating change in her personality compared with how she used to be with him—was painful enough. He didn't understand her anymore, didn't know how to deal with her the way he once did.

He felt her stiffen in his arms, and then her hands slid from around his neck to his chest. Her palms flattened against his pecs—and then she pushed, gently but firmly, and he broke the kiss, his inner caveman berating him for not getting her spread-eagled and naked on the bed.

"We can't do this. Not here." She wouldn't look at him, and that was somehow a hundred times worse than if she had.

"Marry me and we can do it wherever we want."

She closed her eyes and forced out a breath. "That's not what I meant."

"I know." He shrugged, and she blinked at him.

Then she shook her head. "Are you making jokes, Ry?"

He was the joker of the team, but he hadn't felt much humor in the past two months. He still didn't. Jokes were simply a way of hiding pain and insecurity, though most people didn't get that. It had been his coping mechanism as a child, and it still was.

"Maybe I am. But it's also true. Marry me, and no one on earth can stop us from doing what we want to do together."

"Colonel Mendez would have your ass. And you'd lose your job—is that what you want?"

He quite possibly *would* lose his job. Hell, he definitely would. Marrying a known terrorist's widow? A career killer for sure.

"I'll deal with it when it happens."

"Don't you see why I have to stay here? Why I have to finish this mission and find where those hostages are located? Maybe that will be enough to clear my name and let me have a normal life again."

He wanted to go find Ian Black and put a bullet in the fucker's head. "If Colonel Mendez couldn't fix it, what makes you think Black can? You need to realize he's lied to you for his own reasons."

Her brown eyes flashed. "You're so certain of that, aren't you? That Ian lied and that I'm dumb enough to believe him. You can't even entertain the possibility he's telling the truth. But don't you realize what that would mean for me? For *us?*"

He wanted to growl. "Of course I know. But he's a liar, Emily. He's dirty, no matter that he seems to be on the right side at the moment. Ian Black is the kind of man who'll sell his services to the highest bidder—and if you get caught on the wrong side, you'll be the one who suffers."

She shook her head. "I've already suffered—don't

138

you get that? It's a chance I'm willing to take." She put her hand over her belly. "It's a chance I *have* to take."

He looked at her fingers resting on her stomach, and a wave of possessiveness rolled through him like a tsunami. *Mine*. He couldn't stop her, that much was clear. She would fight him every step of the way.

But he could protect her. No, goddammit, he *would* protect her. She was his in a way she never had been before—and he took care of what was his.

He pointed at her. "You aren't going anywhere without me, you got that? You step outside this room, I'm with you. You do an end run around me, and I swear to God, Emily, I'll have your ass bound and gagged and on a plane before you know what hit you. Are we clear on that?"

Her face reddened and her eyes looked like they might bug out of her head. But she kept a rein on her temper for a change. She nodded, a firm, decisive movement that told him she knew he meant business.

Someone knocked on her door and she jumped. Ryan strode over and yanked it open. Brandy was on the other side, his eyes widening as Ryan stood in the entry.

"Am I interrupting?" he asked with an arched brow.

"Yes," Ryan said at the same time Emily said, "No."

Emily came over and pulled the door wider. Ryan let go and stepped back, crossing his arms over his chest and waiting.

"We were just talking," Emily said dismissively. "Have you heard from Victoria?"

"Yeah, had a message a little while ago. She's relieved you're okay. Wants you to come home—and I think she's target practicing for the next time Ian's in town."

Emily snorted. Ryan didn't think Brandy was joking,

however. Or mostly not joking. Soon she'd be practicing with a picture of him as a target too.

"I'll be home soon," she said. "As soon as this mission is over, probably."

Brandy cocked his head, studying her. "Why did you come here in the first place, Em? There were no hostages when you left DC, so why the change of heart now?"

Emily's gaze dropped. "It's hot and dusty here—and I'm tired of it."

"For fuck's sake," Ryan said. "You can't keep it a secret forever."

Emily turned to glare at him. But Brandy's gaze ping-ponged between them. "Keep what a secret? What's going on?"

Ryan thrust his jaw out. Dammit, he didn't want to be her dirty secret. Not when this was so life-altering for them both.

"Don't you dare," Emily grated. "Now's not the time."

"Not the time for what?" Brandy asked, his gaze narrowing.

"She's pregnant," Ryan said, ignoring the daggers she glared at him. "And it's mine."

Emily wanted to kill him. Just wrap her hands around his stubborn throat and squeeze the life from his too-sexy body. Just a few moments ago, she'd been wrapped in his arms, her body pressed against his, and seriously considering ripping his pants open and dropping to her knees before him.

Now she'd like to clobber him.

Nick Brandon looked like someone had clobbered *him*, come to think of it. He gaped at them both. And then the storm clouds rolled in, and Emily could see it coming. The macho asshole was going to have a come-apart. And then Ryan would have a come-apart—and the room would be overrun with testosterone as the two idiots fought over her honor or whatever in the hell they were going to fight about.

"Stop it right now," she said as Nick took a step toward Ryan. "I mean it. No one, and I mean *no one*, is getting into any fights over me or this baby. Ryan, you jerk, you could have kept your mouth shut. And Nick, I know you're only pissed because you know Victoria will be pissed—but honest to God, I'm a grown woman and I can make my own mistakes, so stay the fuck out of this."

Nick didn't look like he was planning to back down—but he didn't move either. His face was a thundercloud.

"Damn right I'm pissed, and not just because of Victoria," he growled. "You're my little sister, or about to be my little sister, and I'm not letting some asshole who can't keep it in his pants take advantage of you."

Ryan laughed. "Jesus, that's rich. You and Victoria couldn't be bothered to pay attention to Emily half the time because you were so damn wrapped up in each other that you forgot she existed."

"I'm going to wipe the floor with you, Flash. Motherfucking wipe the floor and then throw you out like the douche rag you are—"

"Come on, buddy. You fucking try it," Ryan said, stepping closer, opening his arms to give Nick a target.

"No!" Emily yelled as they charged each other like bulls. Somehow she got between them and put her hands on their chests.

They subsided immediately, but their faces were pure fury. She hated that they were ready to come to blows over her. She'd been around HOT for months, on and off, and she knew how close they were. Like brothers. They relied on each other for their lives. They were a well-oiled machine, and they operated behind enemy lines with the complete conviction that each man—or woman—had the backs of every member on their team.

And yet these two were ready to kill each other, and all because of her. Because she'd fallen for Ryan and refused to let him go when she should have. Because she'd gone to him and begged him to break his personal code of honor and make love to her just once.

"It's my fault," she said, her throat tight. "Everything is my fault. And if you two start fighting because of me, I'll feel worse than I already do. So please—*please*—promise me you won't fight."

Neither of them said anything at first. But then Ryan's fingers were on her hand, stroking softly across her skin.

"I won't break Brandy's face, I promise."

Nick grunted. "And I won't break Flash's. Though I want to… and I can't promise that Victoria won't do anything. That one's out of my hands."

"I'll take care of Victoria," Emily said. Though she thanked God her sister was half a world away at the moment. Victoria was one frightening woman when she was angry. Cold, cool, and utterly focused. Not to mention she was one of the best snipers HOT had.

Not that she would lie in wait for Ryan and shoot him dead. Emily shivered. No, she definitely wouldn't do that. But she just might do something pretty scary to put him on notice. Shoot a chunk out of his ear maybe…

"How did this happen?" Nick asked, and Ryan made a noise in his throat that sounded like a warning.

Emily ignored it. "The usual way, I imagine. But before you go telling Victoria that Ryan took advantage of me, you need to know I'm the one who came on to him. He said no. I didn't accept his answer."

"You could have kept saying no, buddy," Nick said, looking over her shoulder at Ryan as if she hadn't said a word and it was all Ryan's fault.

"It's really none of your business," Ryan said. "I don't ask you about your relationship with Victoria, do I?"

"Not the same thing."

"Yeah, it fucking is. Emily is a grown woman. She makes her own choices."

She appreciated him standing up for her. Ryan was the only one who'd seen her as capable of making her own decisions when she'd returned to the States after she'd been rescued. Yes, he'd been there for her and guided her through a few rough moments—but he'd never doubted her ability to choose for herself. Until now, which really pissed her off.

Still, it was one of the reasons she'd fallen for him in the first place.

"So when's the wedding?" Nick asked, and Emily's heart lurched.

"We were working on the details when you interrupted." Ryan spoke mildly, but she could hear the annoyance—and the determination—behind the words.

"We aren't getting married," Emily said. "Ryan asked. I said no. End of story."

"It's not the end of the story," Ryan growled.

Nick put his hands up. "Oookay, guess I've heard enough. I'm out of here."

Emily caught him before he backed out of the room. "You won't tell Vic, will you?"

He gave her a look that said she was crazy. "Honey, I can't hide stuff from her. That's not how it works." He sighed and shook his head. "We're on a mission, so contact isn't regular. I can't message her again for another couple of days. If Black can get a call out for you, you might think about letting her know before I do."

It wasn't much of a reprieve, but it was something. Emily tried not to look visibly relieved. "I'll see if that's possible. Thanks, Nick."

"Sure." He bent to kiss her on the cheek, then glared at Ryan. "You take care of her, Flash."

"That's the plan, asshole."

Nick walked out and Ryan went over to the door. Then he stopped and turned back to her. "I'm gonna get my gear. You better be here when I get back."

Emily's jaw dropped. "You aren't sleeping in here, Ry!"

His expression was hard. "Yeah, I fucking am. I'll sleep on the floor, but I'm not leaving your side. Until you return home, I'm your shadow."

Her throat was tight. "You're on a mission. You have hostages to rescue."

144

"I know that. When it's time to go get them, I'm going. Until then, I'm with you."

"No." She shook her head so hard her hair came loose from the hasty bun she'd put it in. "No way. How do you expect me to explain what you're doing here?"

He snorted. "I don't much care."

"I'm locking the door when you leave."

"Fine. I'll sleep in the hall."

She clenched her fists at her sides. "You're impossible."

"No… I'm determined."

EIGHTEEN

RYAN DIDN'T RETURN FOR ABOUT an hour. Emily had decided he wasn't coming, or maybe Matt had told him no way in hell was he leaving his team to be with her, when there was a knock on her door. She lay on the bed, staring up at the ceiling and thinking about how in the heck she was going to raise a baby, when the sound came.

She didn't move at first. He'd told her he would sleep on the floor in the hall if she didn't let him in—but getting past him in the middle of the night to pee would be hell, that's for sure. Plus, dammit, she just wanted to see him again. She hated herself for the weakness, but there it was.

Emily went over and jerked the door open, gasping when she saw him. Ryan's face wasn't quite the same as when he'd left earlier. His eye was red and swelling, and there was a cut over his lip.

"Nick promised! Are you badly hurt?"

Ryan lifted an eyebrow. "What? No, I'm not hurt."

Emily gritted her teeth. "I'm going to kill him."

"He doesn't look much different. In fact, I think he's currently nursing a bloody nose."

Emily huffed. "You *both* promised. What the hell happened?"

Ryan shrugged. "We're men. He thinks I took advantage of you. I think he's a prick who needs to mind his own business."

Emily went over and sank down on the bed, putting her head in her hands. "I didn't want this. I didn't want you fighting. You and Nick are teammates, brothers. You're supposed to have each other's backs, not kick each other's asses. It's all my fault."

Ryan was at her side, kneeling, pulling her hands away from her face. "We're good, Emily. We just had to get it out of our system, okay? I understand that Nick's going to fight to defend and protect you, and he understands that this is between you and me—and that I'm not going to abandon you to raise this baby alone."

Her stomach flipped. She liked the idea of him being there for her. The idea that he wasn't giving up so easily.

"You don't need to be here, you know. I won't sneak off in the middle of the night. There's nowhere to go."

His blue eyes didn't give anything away. "We're in Ian Black's compound in Acamar. He's a mercenary who deals with some not-very-nice people. There's nothing that says we can't be attacked in the middle of the night."

"No one's raiding this compound, Ryan. The firepower in here is a bit overwhelming, to say the least."

"Maybe so… but you're my responsibility now."

"You really intend to sleep on the floor?"

"Unless you plan to let me into this much-too-narrow bed with you… Yes, I'm sleeping on the floor."

She could insist on throwing him out, but she knew he'd stay in the hallway if she did. Part of her didn't care.

But the other part told her the questions would be worse if he was in the hall. If he was in here, most of the guys wouldn't know or care.

"What did Matt say?"

One corner of Ryan's mouth lifted in a wistful smile. "Did you know Evie's pregnant?"

"Yes. I was there that night at the bar when they announced it."

He pushed a lock of her hair behind her ear. "Yeah, you were, weren't you? So maybe you'll understand when I tell you that Matt gets it. Nothing in heaven or on earth is standing between him and his woman and child."

Emily shivered. *His woman and child.* Such a possessive statement. A sexy statement. She wanted to be Ryan's woman—but she wanted it to be for a reason other than she was pregnant and he had no choice. Still, you got whatever hand life dealt you, not necessarily the one you wanted.

She'd known that from an early age.

"Don't sleep in front of the door."

He cocked an eyebrow. "Why not?"

Emily pushed his shoulder. "I'm pregnant, moron. I have to pee about ten times a night."

"All right." He stood and slung his gear into a corner. Then he unrolled a sleeping bag and laid it on the floor between the bed and the door even though he could have shifted it so the path to the door was free. She'd have to step over him to get out, but at least she could get out.

She suspected he did it that way on purpose, so he'd know whenever she left. She didn't kid herself that he was going to sleep so soundly he wouldn't notice. She'd managed to sneak out of his apartment that night two months ago, but he hadn't been on alert for her movement. To-night, however, she figured he'd know whenever she turned over in bed.

She scooted up against the rickety headboard and watched him. When he pulled off his T-shirt and bared his back to her, she had to bite her lip to keep from groaning. He took off his boots and pants, but he left on a pair of tight navy-blue boxer briefs that hugged the curves of his ass and made her long to reach out and cup those cheeks in her hands.

Emily held her breath as he turned and laid the pants over her chair. He wasn't hard, but there was no mistaking the bulge in his briefs. Her heart skipped a beat, and little beads of sweat formed on her skin. *Oh my goodness...*

His chest was the stuff dreams were made of. Muscles bulged and popped as he moved, and the tribal tattoo on his arm rippled. He had a tattoo on his back as well, an American flag with the HOT badge. Her stomach flipped at the sight of that badge. He was proud of being in HOT, and it worried her to think she might ruin it for him.

Unless Ian gave her half a million dollars and she got the location of the hostages out of Mustafa. Maybe then it would be okay.

She wanted to ask herself who she was kidding, but the truth was she hoped beyond all reason that it worked. Not just for Linda Cooper and the others, but for her and Ryan and their baby.

One thing at a time, Emily.

He turned around again, and she sucked in her breath anew at the sight of his face. When she climbed from the bed and walked toward him, he stopped what he was doing and watched her.

"You need ice."

He gave her a lopsided smile. "Got it, babe."

He reached into his bag and pulled out an instant cold pack. Then he broke it to start the freezing reaction. He waved it at her.

"Want to hold it on my face?"

She folded her arms. "I think you can manage."

He settled onto the floor and lay back on the bed he'd made. Then he put the pack over his eye and glanced at her with the other one. "Yep, guess so."

She returned to her bed and sat down. She was still dressed, but the thought of shucking off her pants and bra and sleeping in nothing but a T-shirt with Ryan so near was paralyzing. Emily reached over and flipped off the lamp, then undressed quickly and got under the sheet. Her nipples tightened as Ryan shifted on the floor.

She thought about how it had felt just an hour ago when he'd kissed her and gently touched her nipples, and her pussy ached with need. If she were alone, maybe she'd do something about it. Instead, she would have to suffer and hope the feelings went away as the night wore on.

The silence between them was thick, tense. In the old days, she would have known what to say, even if she was secretly lusting for him and hoping he might want her too. She'd flirted with him so easily. Chatted with him as if he were her best friend in the world. There'd never been any awkwardness—until the night she'd thrown herself at him.

Everything since then might as well have been happening on a different planet. They weren't the same as they'd been before. She didn't think they ever would be again.

"You all right?"

"Yes," she said automatically. "Why do you ask?"

She could almost feel him shrug. "You're so quiet."

"I'm trying to sleep."

"No, you're not. You're thinking about this baby and how much your life is going to change."

Close. Not that she was telling him what she'd really been thinking about. No way.

Though, dammit, if she did, he'd be up here in two seconds, easing this ache and making her feel wanted, at least temporarily.

Tempting.

"You're quiet too."

"I was waiting for you to say something."

"I'm not the only one with vocal chords, Ry."

"No, you aren't. But I'm not sure what to say to you anymore. Seems like no matter what I say, you get pissed."

Emily sighed. "I get pissed because you're trying to order me around like you're the boss and I'm your subordinate."

"I'm worried about you."

"That's sweet of you, but I'm fine."

"Yeah, so fine you were going out in the city to meet a terrorist while throwing up and getting dizzy. That wasn't bright, honey."

Her skin grew hot. "Jared gave me antinausea meds. I feel much better. And I ate a whole plate of chicken and rice tonight."

"I'm glad to hear it. But that doesn't mean I'm going to stop being concerned."

"You can be concerned all you like. Just don't tell me what to do and we'll be cool."

"Can't promise that."

Emily rolled her eyes even though he couldn't see it. "And I can promise you it will very likely have the opposite effect."

"Meaning you'll do something stupid because I told you not to?"

She wanted to growl. "No... Meaning I'll lose my temper and we definitely will *not* be cool."

"This may surprise you, Emily, but I don't care if we're cool so long as you're safe. If you gotta be pissed at me for trying to protect you, I can deal with that."

She turned on her side and looked at him. The light from outside wasn't strong, but she could see the gleam of his skin whenever he moved.

"I don't want to be pissed at you, Ry. You were my closest friend back in DC."

She could see his arm come up, his hand slide over his head. "So close you left without a word."

"I'm sorry for that. But if I'd told you, you'd have tried to stop me."

"Damn straight. It's dangerous for you to be here."

"So you've said before. And I say it's dangerous for us all."

"Does this Mustafa know who you are?"

Her heart skipped a beat. She could lie, which would be easier, but after a while it got hard to keep lies straight. She'd learned that when she'd been an addict. All the lying and hiding had only made her feel worse.

"He knows."

Ryan swore. "And you've been meeting with him alone this whole time. Goddammit, Emily, don't you have any sense of self-preservation?"

Angry tears threatened, but she swallowed them

down. "I've always had backup. Hassan Mustafa is interested in his bottom line. He's there for the money, not for me."

"Maybe so... but what if someone else in the Freedom Force finds out you're here? What then?"

"We've never tried to hide it," she said. "In fact, I was planning to go inside again."

He sat up so fast she squeaked and scrambled back on the bed in surprise. Her heart raced and she gulped in a breath to calm herself.

"You were planning to infiltrate the Freedom Force? For what fucking purpose, Emily?"

"I was a part of them for three years. I get what's going on in there. I could have helped bring them down from the inside."

"I'm going to kill Black."

She heard the unmistakable click of a weapon being checked, and then Ryan was on his feet. She sprang up and grabbed his arm, her heart ready to burst from her chest.

"Ryan, no! How is this helping anything?" His arm was like granite, hard, immoveable. "If you go after Ian, then you're not protecting me or our baby. You're doing something stupid because you're pissed—just like you've accused me of doing."

He didn't say anything for a long minute. And then the muscles in his arm relaxed and she nearly sobbed in relief.

"I wouldn't have really killed him," he said softly, his voice sounding choked and furious at once. "But I damn sure would have made him wish I had."

"Not helpful, Ry. If you want to protect me... you have to take care of you as well. If you get yourself thrown off this mission, or thrown into a brig back home, how is that helping any of us?"

He let out a breath. Then his hand came up and cupped her head, stroked over her hair. "It's not. But Emily, he doesn't fucking care about you. He'd throw you to the wolves if it suited his purposes."

"I don't believe that." She tumbled on before he could interrupt. "But I do believe he has his own agenda. Absolutely. For your information, I asked him before you arrived what the delay was in sending me in. He said he couldn't do it until he was certain I'd be safe."

"That doesn't make me suddenly like him."

She couldn't help but laugh. "No, I think I know that. But I think you'll have to admit to yourself that he's not quite as evil as you think."

He snorted. They stood there in silence. Ryan kept stroking her hair, and she found herself leaning into his touch.

"I missed you," she said past the sudden lump in her throat. His hand stilled and she wished she could bite her tongue and call the words back.

But then he stroked her hair again and she sighed.

"I missed your texts," he said, and she knew he meant he missed her too. "And your calls."

"Ha, I doubt you missed all of it. I was a mess half the time."

"You'd been through a lot."

"I wasn't your responsibility, but you were always there…" She pulled in a breath. "I've always wanted to ask you something."

"What?"

"Why? Why did you keep answering your phone

when it was me? Why did you spend all that time talking to me and listening to me?"

He took her by the shoulders and guided her back toward the bed. She was confused at first, but he pulled the sheet back and held it for her. She got in, her heart pounding, wondering what he would do next.

But all he did was cover her. Then he holstered the gun and lay back down on the floor. She waited patiently, hoping he would answer but beginning to think he wouldn't. Still, it was a question she'd had for so long, a question she'd been afraid to ask.

Now that she had, she very much wanted to know the answer.

"I told you my parents were divorced," he said. "But I didn't tell you that my mother was bipolar. She didn't always take her meds the way she should. When she was on them, she was great. When she was off... Well, she was dangerous, unpredictable. She had an addictive personality, and she got into drugs."

Emily's heart pinched tight. She knew what it was like to rely on narcotics to make yourself feel better, and she knew what it was like to disappoint those who loved you.

"I'm sorry."

"You don't remind me of her, Emily, if that's what you're thinking. You're strong. She wasn't. But I guess I always thought maybe if I'd been there for her, if I'd listened and tried to help, maybe I could have made a difference." He sighed. "I know that's not true, by the way. I was a child. Maybe if I'd been older... Anyway, when I met you, it was clear you needed someone to listen, someone who wouldn't judge or tell you that you were wrong. I know Victoria loves you, but she was too emotionally invested to listen objectively. I figured I wasn't, so I was perfect for what you needed."

Hearing that he wasn't emotionally invested wasn't quite what she'd hoped to hear. In fact, it made her heart throb with pain.

"You were great, Ry. Probably too great, really. I took advantage of your willingness to listen."

And fell in love with you. Those were the words that hung unspoken between them. She wouldn't say them. They were too hard, too fragile—and she didn't know how she'd handle the inevitable rejection of those words.

Oh, he'd be kind about it. But he would crush her silly dreams at a time when she really couldn't brush it off so easily.

"You didn't take advantage," he said. "I was glad I could be there for you."

"Even if it meant I browbeat you into sleeping with me?" She tried to make it sound humorous, but she was afraid she sounded desperate for validation instead.

"Do you really think that's what happened, Emily?"

"I, uh, well, I didn't leave you much choice."

"Sugar, I always had a choice. I chose the option I wanted the most."

NINETEEN

SHE DIDN'T SAY ANYTHING AND Ryan shifted on the floor. He was used to hard surfaces, used to deprivation and discomfort in the field. He wasn't used to lying on a floor while the woman he wanted lay on a bed only inches away. His body throbbed with heat and need, the same as it had that night in his apartment.

There'd never been a question, not really, of what he would do when faced with Emily's request that he kiss her and make love to her. He'd been half hoping for it for months, and while he'd told himself he wasn't going to do it, that he would be noble and self-sacrificing when and if she ever asked, he'd been doomed to fail from the very beginning.

There was something about Emily. Something that drew him like a plant stretching toward the sun. He could no more walk away from her than he could stop breathing on command.

And that scared him. He wasn't the sort of man to need anyone. He'd learned not to need when he'd been a motherless kid. His father was great, gave him everything

157

a father should—and then some—because the man had the patience of Job. But the other kids had mothers, and he didn't. He knew what a difference that made in their lives, and he'd wanted the same for himself.

Until one day he didn't. Until he'd figured out how to stop needing what he didn't have.

But Emily… Jesus, Emily. Did he need her? Or just want her so badly he couldn't think beyond satisfying a craving?

He didn't know, but he knew that lying here on her floor wasn't good enough. At the same time, if it was all he could have, then it was perfect. Just being near her. Hearing her breathe. Knowing that her heart beat and that a tiny heart inside her body echoed it. A tiny heart that was half him.

"It's sweet of you to say I didn't coerce you," she finally said, "but I think we both know the truth."

He almost rolled his eyes. "Emily, honest to God, do you really think a little bitty thing like you could coerce me into doing anything I didn't want to do? Seriously?"

"You're a man. You'll do anything for sex."

He snorted. "Almost anything. But sugar, I *can* control myself when presented with a delectable female body. I'm not a slave to my dick."

"I played on your feelings of responsibility. I told you I was afraid I'd never be able to be with anyone else."

"Yeah, you did. Even then, I could have refused—I didn't want to, Emily. I wanted you. I'd wanted you for months."

He heard her suck in a breath. "I don't understand why. I was a mess."

"Not to me, you weren't."

To him, she'd been sweet and vulnerable and achingly, forbiddenly beautiful. He'd been fascinated. Drawn to her. Unable to walk away when he should. She'd been a flame, and he'd been the moth attracted to the flame even though he knew he could get burned.

"You don't make any sense sometimes," she said, her voice so quiet in the darkness.

"You can't accept that you're someone I could want, can you? Why is that, Emily?"

It made his chest ache that she could be so uncertain, so blindly stubborn to the truth.

"It's not the physical wanting, Ryan. I get that part…" She sighed. "There's not much I haven't told you about myself… but when I was fifteen, I let a much older man convince me that I was everything to him. It was a lie, as you might imagine, and when Victoria and I were taken from that foster home and sent to another, I thought he'd come for me. That I meant something to him. But of course I didn't. And then there was Zaran… You already know how my relationship with him ended. I think I'm just not someone who inspires commitment—that's what I worry about."

Ryan sat up, his gut churning with anger. He reached for her hand in the darkness, clasped it. "The man who took advantage of you when you were fifteen was a predator. He should have been arrested and charged."

She squeezed his hand. "I know that now. At fifteen, I was desperately in love—and I thought he was too. He was twenty-five, and I thought he was sophisticated. I liked the attention—craved it, actually. When it turned sexual, I didn't feel like I was abused or taken advantage of. I felt special, grown-up. But it didn't last, and when he didn't come for me, I was devastated." She snorted. "As only a teenager in love can be, you know?"

"I'm sorry, Emily."

"I know, and I appreciate it."

"Just because some asshole sexual predator took advantage of your feelings, and just because Zaran lost his mind, doesn't mean there's anything wrong with you. Tell me you understand that."

"I… I don't know. Honestly, I wonder. Except for my sister, I've been alone my whole life. The times I thought I wasn't, the times I thought I'd found someone who would love me for who I am, I was wrong. And with Zaran…"

He knew what she didn't say. She'd put a knife into Zaran's gut in order to survive, and that wasn't an easy thing to live with, especially since she'd once loved him. Ryan climbed onto the bed and put his arms around her. She turned and burrowed into his chest, her fingers resting on his skin. Burning into him like hot steel even while her words chilled him.

"There's nothing wrong with you, honey. You're an amazing woman. A strong woman. And *I* care about you." He couldn't say *love*. He didn't know what that felt like— but he knew what caring felt like. And he knew that he did. "I care about our baby. Nothing you do or don't do can change that."

She laughed softly. "Oh, Ryan, you're the sweetest thing. But you don't really know that. You don't know how you'd feel if you had to leave HOT because of me."

"Goddammit, Emily." He tipped her chin up in the darkness. He could see her face in the dim light coming from outside, the glitter of her eyes. Her breathing was quick, and he knew her pulse must be racing. "Don't you understand that people are more important than things? HOT is a thing. If I have to leave, I'll be fine. *We'll* be fine. I'll still have the Army—and if I don't, if they ask me to leave that too, I'll find something to do. I have skills."

It hit him then that the skills he had would be perfect for Ian Black's outfit. Not that he wanted to work for Black. Hell, maybe he'd start his own mercenary security outfit. There was no shortage of need for that kind of thing in the world.

"I don't want you to end up hating me." Her voice was a whisper, but he could hear the wealth of pain in it. Pain caused by her childhood and by her asshole husband who'd blamed her for not being able to get pregnant. If Zaran bin Yusuf weren't already dead, Ryan would take great pleasure in putting him six feet under.

"I'm not going to hate you, honey."

Her fingers curled against his chest. "You don't know that. I never thought Zaran would change, but he did."

"We all change." In the back of his mind, he thought of his mother, of her sickness. Yeah, he'd wondered if that sickness would affect him, but he'd made it this far in life without any signs of it, so he figured he was going to be okay. "But that kind of change—it wasn't normal, Emily. You know it wasn't."

They'd talked about it before, about how Zaran had seemed ordinary at first, about how he'd helped Emily get clean and seemed to worship her. But when he'd gotten involved with radicals, he'd changed, become obsessed with his own grandeur. The truth was that he'd been a narcissist, and his attention on Emily at first, his insistence on helping her get clean, was simply a way of controlling her. He'd used her as a reflection of himself—a *look what I did* moment he could trot out for others as an example of how wonderful he was. It had never been about helping Emily. It had been about glorifying himself.

"You're right… but it still bothers me."

"You'd be inhuman if it didn't."

"I know you care, Ryan. And I… I care about you. But you have to understand why I can't just hand my life over and hope for the best."

He did understand. He didn't like it, but he got it. He leaned back against the headboard and crossed his ankles, pulling her more securely against his body. She lay against him, one arm over his middle. She felt good there. Right.

He didn't know what else to say to her, how to convince her he wasn't giving up on her. So he feathered his lips over her forehead and stroked her hair off her cheek.

"Go to sleep, Emily. I've got you."

It was still dark when Emily awoke. She was crowded in the bed and she didn't understand why at first. But then she realized her cheek lay against warm skin and her arm was slung across a hard body.

Ryan's body. He lay beside her, his chest rising and falling evenly. She peered up at him, but his eyes remained closed. She shifted slightly and instantly knew what had woken her up.

She had to pee. Damn.

She liked lying in Ryan's arms, his warm body next

to hers, his breathing even and steady. She was comforted by it and she didn't want to move.

But she had to, or she'd make this night a memorable one for them both. Emily levered herself up carefully, intending to somehow climb over him and escape to the bathroom without waking him.

"Where are you going?" His voice was gravelly as he shifted in the bed.

"I have to go to the bathroom."

He swung his legs over the edge to make room for her, and she clambered out of bed and onto the floor.

"Promise you aren't running away, Emily."

"I'm wearing a T-shirt and panties. I'm not running away."

"A T-shirt and panties? Not only did I not need to hear that, but I also think you should put on some clothes before you go out in the hall."

"I have a robe." She grabbed the robe from where she'd slung it over the foot of the bed and slipped it on.

"It's not a short robe, right? Nothing sexy?"

"It's knee-length and no, I don't think it's sexy. I also don't think it's any of your business." She pretended to be annoyed, but really she was kind of amused. It was the middle of the night, she was pregnant and had to pee, and he was worried about her being sexy as she walked down the hall.

"Need me to come with you?"

"Like you have every night since I've been here, right?"

"No need to get testy."

"I'm not testy. I'm just pointing out the ridiculousness of your thinking I need an escort to the bathroom."

He sighed. "Fine, I'm ridiculous. Now hurry up and get back here. It's cold without you lying against me."

She tried not to let those words mean too much, but the truth was they made her feel a little twinge of happiness. Then again, she thought of their conversation before she'd fallen asleep, and fresh uncertainty filled her. She wanted to believe they could be happy in spite of the circumstances bringing them together, but she was too jaded to let herself really imagine it.

She knew what it was like when the person you thought you knew became someone else entirely. Not that she expected Ryan to change so drastically, but any man forced into taking care of a family he hadn't expected was going to be frustrated as time went on. Because babies didn't get easier. She knew that much.

Emily finished her business and returned to the bedroom. The compound was quiet for the most part, though she knew Ian was probably going over plans in his office and of course there were guys on patrol.

Ryan was convinced it wasn't safe here, but it was so quiet and ordinary to her that it felt perfectly normal. She closed the door softly, thinking maybe he'd fallen asleep while she'd been gone, but he moved as she approached and flipped the sheet back.

She climbed over him and settled into the mattress again.

"Everything okay?"

"Yes, fine. The meds helped tremendously. I don't feel sick anymore—just tired and hungry."

"Are you hungry now?"

"Maybe a little."

He slipped from the bed and started to tug on his

pants. "I'll find something."

"You don't have to do that, Ry. It'll be breakfast soon."

"You don't have to wait, Emily."

She curled up against the headboard while he disappeared through the door. Emily yawned and turned her head into the pillow. It smelled like Ryan, and she inhaled deeply. In reality, she'd never thought to have his scent on her pillow after the way she'd left him in DC. She'd known when she walked out of his apartment that night that she might never see him again.

To see him now—to be in the same bed with him, even if it was only platonic—was more heaven than she'd dreamed possible here in her tiny room in Acamar.

A few minutes later, the door opened and he walked in with a tray he'd scrounged. Her heart flipped and squeezed. Would it always hurt like this to see him? It wasn't a bad hurt, but it was a hurt nonetheless. She loved him desperately, but she had to be cautious because she knew what happened when her love wasn't returned. How sickening and disappointing it felt.

Emily sat up as he came over and put the tray over her lap.

"You need the light?"

"No, I can see."

There was some of that marvelous grilled flatbread that came with all the meals, fresh grapes, and some cheese.

"It's not much, but it's what I could easily get my hands on." He produced a bottle of water and Emily took it, her heart swelling out of proportion to the act. Sheesh, he was being nice the way he'd always been. It was nothing more than that. She could *not* read more into any of his actions, even if circumstances had changed between them.

"It's perfect. I'm not sure how much I can eat, though."

He sat beside her again, and her pulse skidded higher. "Eat what you can."

"I guess I should be thankful I didn't crave ice cream," she said with a laugh as she broke off a piece of bread and popped it in her mouth.

"Yeah, I'm not sure I could have found ice cream at this hour. I've noticed an appalling lack of Walgreens stores on street corners."

"I kinda look forward to getting back home and having twenty-four-hour HGTV again."

"HGTV, huh? I don't think I realized you liked watching home shows."

"There's just something about people shopping for houses that I like. Especially when they complain about the paint color or the fact there's only one toilet. I just want to tell them they're lucky to have a toilet, so shut the eff up, you know?"

"Most people don't realize how good they have it."

She ate a piece of cheese. "No, they really don't. Three years in desert camps would shock most of them into heart failure." She put the cheese down. "I hope Linda Cooper is okay. She has to be so stressed right now—and that's not good for the baby."

"We're going to get them out, Emily."

"I know you will. I just need to find them for you."

He reached over and skimmed his fingers along the back of her hand. "We'll find them. If we're lucky, Mendez will know something soon—and you won't have to meet Mustafa again."

If she never had to look at Hassan Mustafa's face again, she'd be thrilled. But somehow she didn't think it was going to end that easily. She'd meet him, carrying half a million in cash, and pray he really knew where the hostages were. She fully expected him to lie about it—but then so did everyone here.

He could lie, so long as he knew their true location. Because he would share it, of that she had no doubt. Willingly or unwillingly, he'd spill before it was over. HOT would make sure he did.

"I hope that's true. Still, I'll go if I have to."

"I know that."

She looked up at him. "You won't try to stop me?"

His eyes glittered in the darkness. "Didn't say that."

She reached for him, her fingers landing on one rock-hard pec, her palm flattening against smooth skin. "You can't interfere, Ry. The hostages… Their lives, the baby's life—"

Her voice choked off and he caught her hand, dragged it to his mouth. "I won't interfere, Emily—unless your life is in danger. You come first with me, you got that?"

She nodded, the lump in her throat too tight to speak. He turned her hand over and kissed her palm. When his tongue touched the center, she gasped—but she didn't pull away. Instead, she brought her other hand up and laid it against his jaw, her fingers trembling at the emotion running through her.

She always felt so much with this man. Too much. The veil over her feelings was incredibly thin with him.

He turned his head and kissed her other hand and she cupped his cheek. It was rough with stubble that scraped her palm.

"Think I need to get back on the floor," he muttered, grasping her elbows and gently removing her hands from his face.

Emily swallowed the hard knot in her throat. Her body ached, her skin was on fire, and her breasts tingled. Being left alone in this bed suddenly felt like the end of the world. She craved connection with him, even if it was temporary. Closeness.

"What if I don't want you to leave?"

TWENTY

EVERY CELL IN RYAN'S BODY stood at attention. His cock grew harder, if that was possible. His brain warred with his dick and the primal urge he had to push her back on the bed and bury himself inside her willing body.

"I want to stay. I want to strip you naked and lick every inch of your body. I want to make you come so hard you won't remember your name—and then I want to do it all again."

His voice was a growl, and Emily's breath hitched.

"But you're fragile right now, and I'm not sure it's the best idea," he finished before she could say anything.

She shook her head. "Oh Ryan, you are the most amusing man sometimes."

Hell, he was amusing a lot of the time. But this time wasn't one of them—or so he'd thought. "I'm not being funny."

"Yes, you definitely are." She reached for him again, stroked her soft fingertips along the roughness of his cheek. "I'm pregnant, not dying. Pregnant women have sex."

He caught her hand and pressed it over his pec, holding it there. Feeling the brand of her skin against his. The sweet heat.

"How would you know? How would I?" He was kidding this time, but he knew she'd decide he was being serious.

"I know because I'm a woman. And I can read and write and everything, Ryan."

He snorted. "Who's being amusing now?"

"Ask a stupid question…"

"All right, so it was a stupid question. But Em… you weren't exactly happy with me earlier."

"I don't have to be happy with you to want you. And you're right, I wasn't happy. You had no business telling Nick I'm pregnant. I'm still not happy about that."

He rubbed a hand over his face. Yeah, he'd gone full caveman on that one. "Thought you'd moved on from that."

"Nope, sure didn't. I was too tired to argue about it when you came back. I'm awake now."

He wasn't sure why he'd said it, except that he'd had this possessive urge to claim her and their baby. To let everyone know that she was his and he was taking care of her.

"I'm tired of pretending there's nothing between us," he said. "I'm tired of hiding from everyone and acting like you're a stranger."

She stroked her hand down his chest, back up again. His body reacted to her touch as if someone had set off a nuclear reaction in his core. It was everything he could do not to move, not to strip the T-shirt from her body and lick his way down to her pussy.

"It's better for you that way," she said. "Safer for your job."

"Yeah, well, I'm changing the rules. I don't fucking care about that anymore. I care about you, about us and this baby. You're my priority, Emily. Don't you get that?"

Her head dropped. "I'm trying. It's hard for me."

"I know." He blew out a breath. "I want you so much, but I want to prove to you that this isn't just about sex. Which is why I'm returning to the floor."

"You'd deprive us both of comfort just to prove a point?"

His heart thumped. "You aren't making this easy."

"I don't intend to."

Her hand slipped down to his groin, rubbed him through the pants that were too tight across his cock now. He couldn't stop the groan that left his throat.

"You want this," she said. "So do I."

"Jesus, you're a hard woman to say no to. Brandy was right that I should have kept saying no—but I didn't want to. I don't want to now either."

"So don't. I need you, Ryan. I need to know that you're with me, that you care the way you say you do."

He let out a choked laugh. "If I didn't know better, I'd say you're the player in this situation and I'm the virgin you're trying to seduce."

She laughed. "You are so far from a virgin it's not funny."

He took the tray from her lap and set it on the floor. While he was twisted away from her, she took the opportunity to climb over him and settle with her crotch riding his erection. He gripped her hips and held her against him, flexing his body so he pressed into her most sensitive spot.

"Oh," she gasped, wriggling her hips against him. "Oh Ryan, that feels amazing."

His head pounded. His heart throbbed. And his cock ached to be inside her.

"You make it impossible to say no."

"Good."

He slid his hands from her hips, let his thumbs do the walking down to the vee of her legs. Her panties were wet as he rubbed his thumbs over the soft cotton.

"I've never been with a pregnant woman before," he murmured.

She snorted. "Makes two of us. I've never been pregnant before."

"Don't want to hurt the baby."

She moaned a little when he kept stroking his thumbs over her panties, pressing against her clit. "You won't. The baby is oblivious in his own little world."

"His, huh?"

"I don't know that for sure. Just taking a guess."

He gripped her again and turned them both until he was on top and she lay beneath him with her legs around his waist.

"You make me hot, Emily. Always have. But this... this idea that you're carrying my baby in there... I'd take a bullet for you both. I'd endure the worst kind of torture to keep you safe. I'd let the Freedom Force have me before I let them have you."

She popped a hand over his mouth. "Don't say things like that. Please don't. I can't stand the thought of anything happening to you, and certainly not because of me."

He kissed her palm, pulled it away. "Don't worry, honey. They aren't getting me—and they damn sure aren't getting you. We'll finish this mission and we'll go home. We'll figure it out, okay?"

She nodded. Her other hand came up and threaded into his hair. "Please kiss me. I'll die if you don't kiss me."

Fuck. He already knew he was lost. Already knew he wasn't getting out of this bed without thoroughly making love to the woman beneath him. She stole his ability to reason. If she didn't, she wouldn't be pregnant, would she?

But right now, he just didn't fucking care. All he cared about was getting inside her, taking her with him on a hot, sensual journey that would make the world fade into nothingness.

"Whatever you want, honey. Whatever you need."

Ryan dropped his mouth to hers and found heaven.

Emily's heart threatened to beat out of her chest as Ryan kissed her. Their tongues danced and tangled, and Ryan's cock swelled. Emily shifted her hips and ground herself against him, wanting more of the sweet pressure against her clit that he'd been giving her with his thumbs.

She was primed, hot and ready. It surprised her how much she wanted this, how desperate she was to join her body with his. She'd been angry with him, frustrated with his stubbornness and his lack of confidence in her ability to do a job.

But now—oh, now—she didn't care about any of that. Her body ached with desire. Her core tightened and her pussy grew even wetter if that was possible.

Ryan shoved her T-shirt up and off, then backed away and yanked her panties down, sliding them over her legs until she was naked beneath him. She lay there trembling, wondering what he would do next. When he only sat above her without moving, she reached for the button at his waist. He hadn't removed his pants when he'd returned from the kitchen, and she wanted them off.

"In a minute," he growled, dropping down and putting his hands beneath her ass, spreading her wide.

"What are you doing?" As if she didn't know.

His eyes twinkled wickedly. "Honey, I'm about to eat your pussy. You need a good licking."

Emily gasped as his fingers slid up the wet seam of her cleft.

"Better put that pillow over your face to muffle the screams," he continued. "Or everyone in this compound's going to know what you're up to in here."

It was unbelievable that he could make her blush—but he managed it. Her skin was hot. "Oh, you're bad!"

"So bad I'm good, baby. Hold on." Ryan's tongue slipped into her wet heat and she grabbed the pillow out of instinct.

Then he licked his way from the bottom to the top, and she turned her face into the pillow as instructed. When his tongue curled around her clit, she moaned long and low.

"Ryan, please."

"Please what, Emily?"

"Please stop torturing me!"

He chuckled. "Torturing you? I've barely started. I've licked your sweet pussy twice."

Twice? Only twice? God, she would never survive this.

"You haven't done anything but tease!"

"That's right, baby." He dropped his head again and licked the swollen folds of her pussy. His tongue dipped inside her again, tasting and teasing, and she rocked her hips up, hoping for more.

But he laughed and pulled away. Then his tongue flattened over her clit, pressing into the bundle of nerves, and she made a noise very much like a whimper. No, it *was* a whimper. Hell.

Next he curled his tongue around her clit again, flicking it hard and soft, hard and soft, until she thought she might scream.

So, yes, she balled up the pillow into her fists, and she pressed her face into it—because the sounds coming from her, while not especially loud, were somewhat embarrassing. And had the potential to go up a few octaves if he didn't stop.

Which she didn't want him to do. Never stop. *Never stop.*

Ryan spread her with his fingers, opening her for better access, his tongue flicking faster against her clit now. The tension inside her body grew taut, ready to explode—

And Ryan stopped what he was doing and moved down to thrust his tongue inside her again. Just when she thought she might scream with frustration and yes, even pleasure, he went back to her clit. This time he sucked it into his mouth, sucked almost too hard, but not really.

It was mind-blowing, skating on the edge of pleasure and pain. Not pain because it hurt, but pain because it was *too* good. Too intense.

He flicked her clit while sucking, and Emily squeezed the pillow tighter. She was about to blow. About to come apart in this tiny bed in the middle of a compound full of hardened warriors. Sure, some of them were probably having sex now too—there were women here, though not many—but she could hardly care about them when she was so close to heavenly bliss.

She kept one hand on the pillow while she reached down and put the other on the back of his head, pressing his face into her pussy. She felt him smile, felt the rumble of a chuckle in his throat—

The vibrations—and his wickedly good tongue—sent her sailing off the edge. Her body shook, her legs trembled, her breath caught in her throat. Her back arched, her breasts thrusting into the air. Ryan reached up and pinched one of her nipples gently, and she nearly zoned out.

Oh my God, it was so good. So intense. More intense than the first night with him, and that had been pretty incredible.

She moaned her pleasure into the pillow—hell, maybe she screamed it. She wasn't certain. Ryan kept licking her until she let him go. Then he kissed his way up her body to her breasts, sucking her nipples into his mouth one after the other.

They were so sensitive her back arched and she gasped as she felt the tug of sensation all the way to her pussy, her toes. She shoved the pillow out of her face so she could breathe.

"Why are you still wearing pants?" she asked when she could manage to speak.

"Because I'm taking care of you."

"They need to go, Ryan."

176

He rolled to the side and laughed as he flicked a button open. She reached for him, helping him unbutton his fly before he kicked the pants down his legs and off. She'd forgotten he was wearing briefs, but she went after those, pushed them down until he could kick them off as well.

"You're kinda insatiable right now, you realize that?"

"Yes. Are you complaining?"

"Hell no. What kind of man complains about a woman wanting his dick?"

"Exactly." She reached for him, wrapped her hand around the smooth, hard flesh of his cock. "I definitely want this. I want you."

She said the last a little shyly, which was silly considering what he'd just done to her. But she was shy with him. Shy in the sense that her heart was so engaged and she knew his wasn't. She was afraid, afraid of what sex with him meant to her—and yet she needed it too. She couldn't walk away. Couldn't say no.

Didn't want to say no.

Ryan rose above her, settled himself between her legs. And then he paused, looking down at her while she held his cock and tried to guide him into her body.

"I want you to know that I realize what a gift this is," he said softly. "Your body. Your pleasure. I'm thankful you chose me."

Her heart felt like it might crack wide open and spill all her feelings out into the air between them. She swallowed hard, unwilling to let that happen. Sex was one thing, but love would surely make him think twice.

"This isn't the time to make me cry," she whispered.

He grinned. "Not unless you're crying my name, sweetheart."

Before she could think up an appropriate answer, the head of his cock slid inside her slick walls.

"We good?"

She blinked up at him. "You aren't even there yet. Barely there. Of course we're good!"

"Hey, for all I know, you're supersensitive now that you're pregnant."

"I am—in my nipples. This is all good—and that little bit of you is a huge tease."

"Huge. I like the sound of that."

"Ryan."

"Yeah, baby?"

"This isn't the time to make jokes."

"Honey, I'm hurt. You saying my cock isn't huge after all?"

She wrapped her legs tighter around his waist and tried to pull him into her by force. It didn't work because he was much bigger and way stronger than she was. She growled at him.

"Stop teasing me, Ryan!"

He slid deeper inside her, her body stretching to accommodate him. No, he definitely wasn't small. The walls of her pussy gloved him tight, but it wasn't uncomfortable.

"Still good?" He didn't sound so humorous now. He sounded… strained.

"Yes. Still good. Please, please finish it."

He reached down and put a hand under her ass, lifting her to him—and then he slid home and they both groaned.

"God, that's good," he said.

"Yeah… wow."

He pulled out and pushed back inside her again and again, slowly, until she made a sound of frustration. The next time he slammed into her a little harder.

"Yessss…"

That was pretty much all he needed to hear, because he started moving harder now, faster, driving her deep into the mattress. The bed frame was old and it squeaked like crazy.

She didn't care. She also didn't care that she was moaning his name, begging him for more. He took her mouth, kissed her deeply, his tongue like hot velvet. They moved frantically, bodies slamming together, bed rocking, hips meeting forcefully with each thrust.

If she could get closer to him, she would. If she could be a part of him, she would. But this had to be enough, this beautiful melding of two sweat-slick bodies.

"Ryan, Ryan…"

"I'm here, Emily. I'm with you."

He reached between them, found the sensitive pearl of her clit, stroked it in rhythm to the way he pounded into her. She gripped him tight, her hands raking down his back, grasping hard muscle and hot skin.

And then she flew apart, her orgasm hitting her like a truck she didn't see coming. She might have screamed. She might have sworn. She didn't know what she'd done except that she knew she was coming hard and it wasn't over yet.

"Fuck me," Ryan muttered. "That's beautiful, Emily. So damn beautiful. Keep coming just like that."

She did, even as he withdrew and slammed into her again and again, not letting her down from the high, not giving her an ounce of reprieve. Her pussy squeezed him tight, gripped him hard, increasing the friction until he lost control of his response.

She knew he was coming by the way he stiffened, by the way his hips jerked into hers. The cords of his neck were tight as he threw his head back. He withdrew a couple of inches and then slammed back into her, his cock jerking as he came. She felt the hot wash of his semen inside her.

Even while he came, he still managed to continue stroking her clit, eliciting even more pleasure from her body.

"That was fucking amazing," he finally said when she'd stopped shaking, her limbs too tired to even tremble. He withdrew, his cock still hard, and then surged forward again.

It still felt amazing, even if she was spent.

"I want to stay right here forever," he told her. "Right here deep inside you. My cock and your pussy, together forever."

She couldn't help but giggle. "Joined at the groin, huh? What about food and drink?"

He dropped a kiss onto her shoulder, her collarbone. "I don't care. Someone can bring us food and drinks. We'll fuck all the time, and we'll be blissfully happy."

"I think the baby might want out at some point."

"Yeah, probably so. We'll stop for that. Soon as he's out, we're fucking again."

She pushed his shoulder. He made her blush and he made her want him all at the same time. "You're silly. No one fucks twenty-four seven."

He licked a path around one of her nipples and she gasped. "Maybe they should. The world would be a better place if everyone was more concerned with fucking each other and less concerned with other things."

"Can't argue with that. But unfortunately not everyone is as enlightened as you are, Ryan."

"As *we* are, honey."

"Right. *We.*" She sighed and pushed her fingers through his hair. It was damp and curly, and she loved that she had the right to touch him like this. What would it be like if she could touch him like this every day for the rest of her life?

Her heart flipped. If she married him…

But, no, if she married him and he was only doing it for the baby's sake, then it wasn't the same thing at all. Because he would resent her eventually. Resent that she'd trapped him into marriage.

You don't know that.

No, she didn't—but she knew that a marriage built on duty wasn't quite the same thing as one built on passion and love for each other. He hadn't yet said he loved her. She hadn't said it either—but why would she? She was terrified to do so.

"I'm still hard…"

"I noticed."

He sucked a nipple between his lips and she moaned, clutching his head to her body. Fresh excitement began to build inside her core, rolling outward in waves of sizzling heat. If she couldn't have his love, at least she could have this.

"You feel like coming again?" he asked as he trailed his mouth over to her other nipple.

"Yes… definitely, yes…"

"Me too. Hold on, Emily. It's about to get crazy in here…"

TWENTY-ONE

"MORNING, FLASH."

"Morning." Ryan picked up a plate and dished out some eggs. No bacon, dammit, because this was Acamar and pork wasn't allowed.

Fiddler watched him with a lifted brow as he approached. The dude knew something was up, but Ryan wasn't telling him exactly what. The other guys barely glanced up from their plates other than to nod. They'd all been witness to the fight he'd had with Brandy. They might not know the whole reason, but they knew Emily was at the center of it.

"Missed you last night," Fiddler said.

Ryan forked up some eggs. "Missed you too, baby doll."

Fiddler snorted. "Asshole."

"Is that what you missed about me, sweetie?"

Fiddler tossed a piece of bread at him. Ryan gave him a grin and put the bread on his own plate. Man, he was tired. And his back ached. Emily's bed was too fucking narrow for two people. Or three, if you wanted to be technical about it.

But goddamn, he wouldn't trade a second of last night for more comfort. When he'd insisted on sleeping on her floor, he hadn't expected he'd spend a good part of the night in her bed. Or in her body.

Fuck, what a night. What a damn night. His body was tired in all the right ways, but it wouldn't take much to get him hard again. Just thinking about Emily would do the trick if he wasn't careful.

Brandy walked into the room then. His face didn't look much better as he grabbed a plate and filled it. Then he came over and sat across from Ryan. Not an accident, that.

"How you doing this morning, Flash? Sleep good?"

Ryan forked more eggs into his mouth. "Never better. You?"

"She agree to marry you yet?"

Fiddler's head swung toward Brandy. A couple of the other guys nearby overheard and looked up as well.

"I'm working on it."

"Why won't she agree to marry you, dude? She can't get any more knocked up than she already is."

"Whoa, man," Fiddler said. "Emily's pregnant? You got her pregnant?"

Ryan's good mood was fast evaporating. But he'd started this, hadn't he? Last night, when he'd insisted on telling Brandy against Emily's wishes. Shit. He was feeling about two inches tall right now, especially when Emily walked into the room then, her long blond hair tied back in a ponytail, that gorgeous body he'd worshipped encased in a black utility jumpsuit. It wasn't a sexy garment, but on her it was. It hugged her breasts, tapered to her waist, and then flared over her hips like a lover's caress.

She stopped and stared at him. Or maybe at the table of men who were currently staring back at her.

Ryan shot to his feet and went to her side, drawn to her like she'd reeled him in. Maybe she had.

She looked up at him, her brown eyes softening, her cheeks growing pink. "Hi."

"Hi. How do you feel this morning?"

"Much better." She glanced behind him, presumably at his team, and then lowered her voice. "Maybe a little sore. But in a good way."

Fuck. He had to fight not to get hard when she said that, because every single memory of last night scrolled through his head like a dirty movie. A hot, sexy, sweet, dirty movie in which they'd been the two stars.

"Sorry about that."

Her gaze sharpened. "I'm not… Okay, want to tell me why all the guys are staring?"

"Brandy said something about us getting married."

Her eyes shuttered. "We aren't getting married."

"Not arguing about that with you right now, but I'm not done with the subject." He reached for her hand, clasped it in his. "Brandy might have mentioned the reason we need to get married."

Her jaw tightened. "Well, shit. Why'd he go and do that?"

"Because he's pissed at me. And he cares about you." Ryan drew in a breath. "But it's my fault. He wouldn't know if I hadn't said something in the first place."

She didn't let go of his hand. Instead, she turned it over and looked at the back of it. Then she looked up at him. "I only wanted to protect you. It wasn't about hiding from anyone. I'm not ashamed of you, Ryan. You have to know that."

He knew she was concerned about his place on the team, about what the colonel would say when he found out. But it was odd to hear her say she'd wanted to protect him when that was his job. Protecting her. Keeping her safe.

"I know. But you let me worry about me, okay? You've got enough to worry about with the baby. I need you healthy. *He* needs you healthy."

Her smile was soft. "Or she."

"Yeah, or she. I don't much care so long as everything is okay." He tipped his chin at the food. "Why don't you sit down and let me get it?"

"I can manage, Ryan," she said, her eyes sparkling with humor now. "Save it for when I look like I've got a bowling ball in my belly."

She peered over his shoulder, her expression firming. Then she tugged him back toward the long table where his team, and much of Echo Squad, sat. When they got there, she didn't let go of his hand.

"Yes," she said to no one in particular, "I'm pregnant. Yes, Ryan is the father. No, it's none of your business what happens between us. If we get married, you'll all be invited to the ceremony. And if we don't, you'll still be invited to the baby shower. Is that enough for you jerks, or do you need more details?"

There was coughing and the shuffling of feet.

"Uh, congratulations," Fiddler said. "I'm good."

"Yep, good," Dexter "Double Dee" Davidson replied. Knight Rider and Big Mac echoed him.

Iceman stood up and came over to give her a quick

hug. "Congrats," he said. "Babies are awesome."

Billy the Kid tipped his chin. "Awesome news. Congrats."

Matt's grin was huge. "Our kids can play together," he said. "Evie's going to be excited as hell."

Echo Squad's guys merely shrugged and offered their congratulations. Brandy was the only one who looked kinda confused. Then he stood and offered his hand to Ryan. They stood there for a long moment, neither speaking, the tension in the air evident.

"You take care of her, Flash. She deserves the best you've got."

"I know that, man. It's what I intend to do."

They exchanged a long look that Ryan knew had little to do with Emily being pregnant and everything to do with the idea she was planning to meet with Hassan Mustafa while carrying half a million in cash. Neither of them wanted that meeting to take place.

Ryan gave his head a small shake to signify he understood, and Brandy nodded. They dropped the handshake, and Ryan made room for Emily at the table. She went back to the food line to get her breakfast, and Ryan met Brandy's gaze again. Then he turned to Matt, who was farther down the table.

"Any word from HQ about the hostages?"

"The analysts are studying satellite images of the Lost City from the night the abduction happened. They're hoping for a trail that leads them to where the hostages are being kept."

Desert sands shifted, but there could be something from the night the hostages were taken. A heat signature leading in a certain direction perhaps. They could then plot out the coordinates of the path and see where it led.

Matt's gaze met his, then shifted to Brandy. "We're doing the best we can to find them before tomorrow's meeting."

He glanced at Emily, who was currently preoccupied with filling her plate and talking to the dude who'd been with her yesterday when she'd gone to meet Mustafa. Ryan had watched that meeting from across the street, his muscles straining with the effort not to go to her side. She'd handled herself just fine—but he didn't trust Hassan Mustafa or his motives.

"She can't go to that meeting, Richie. It's too dangerous."

"I know, *mon ami*. We'll get it worked out."

Ryan nodded and turned his attention back to Emily as she strode toward him, a soft smile on her face when their gazes met. His heart flipped and his gut churned with fresh need and possessiveness.

Whether they worked it out or not, he wasn't letting her go to that meeting.

"Any idea who this Raja could be?"

Emily glanced up at Ian. She was sitting in his office, having her daily briefing and not paying half as much attention as she should to what he was saying. But she had been thinking about Raja—when she wasn't totally overwhelmed by Ryan, that is.

"Not really. The women I knew weren't involved in the organization any more than I was. We were wives, nothing more. Not fit for anything other than gracing our husband's beds and taking care of their domestic needs."

"No, the Freedom Force has never been a woman-friendly outfit, have they?"

"Understatement. They'd like to take away any and all rights woman have gained in the Arab world. Women should be veiled, silent, and biddable."

"Yet Zaran taught you to shoot."

Her grandfather had wanted to teach her. He'd taught Victoria—but then he'd died, and she'd never learned until Zaran taught her.

"I think it amused him. Plus I'm American." Zaran had let her listen in during his meetings sometimes. He'd liked talking about himself, and it was much easier to do that if she was a witness to his greatness. At the time, she'd felt special. Now she knew it was really all about him.

And she'd never been a witness to any discussions involving terror attacks. She liked to think she would have escaped somehow if that had been the case. No, she'd just thought that Zaran was a revolutionary, an intellectual. Until it was too late and she'd realized that he was fighting for more than Qu'rimi independence.

She toyed with a pen she'd taken from Ian's desk, flipping it up and down on her leg. "I don't know that a woman could come from the outside, though, and enter at such a level. It would need to be someone who was already in the inner circle. And I wasn't privy to the highest echelons of the organization—but I could see perhaps a wife of a powerful man taking control if something happened to him."

"Supreme control though. That's pretty astounding."

"It definitely is. I don't know who could have accomplished it. I met many of the women, and none struck me as being so cold-blooded they could manage it. On the other hand, when faced with the loss of a lifestyle, who knows what someone is capable of?"

Ian looked thoughtful. "Yes, this is certainly true." He leaned back on his chair and fixed her with a look that she would have said contained more than a modicum of concern. "So, the rumor is you're pregnant. Is it true?"

It took her a second to recover. Of course the truth was running rampant around the compound now, but she would have thought Jared would have told Ian right away. Clearly he hadn't.

"Yes, it's true."

"Planning to continue the pregnancy?"

It was a legitimate question, but it stunned her nevertheless. Ian didn't know what she'd gone through with Zaran—that this baby was not only a surprise, but something of a miracle to her.

"I am. Which means I'll need to go back to the States soon, I suppose."

Ian's dark eyes gave nothing away. "I suppose so… Is Ryan Gordon the father?"

"He is… why the twenty questions, Ian?"

He shrugged. "I'd like to know what I'm dealing with when tomorrow comes."

"He won't interfere with the meeting. It's too important, and he knows it."

"That's good."

Emily sucked in a breath and asked the question she'd

been dreading. "Will this be enough for me? Will you clear my name?"

Ian's expression didn't change. "I don't know, Emily. It's not up to me. I'll do what I can... but there are no guarantees. I think my contacts expected you to be with us a bit longer. Your knowledge is valuable."

Her heart thumped. "Yes, and I still have it. Just because I go back to DC doesn't mean I can't be useful somehow."

"I'll pass that on. But no promises, Emily. I can't give you false hope."

Frustration hammered her. "I've done a lot. I've gotten Mustafa to trust me, and he's given us good information in the past two months. I would have liked to have gone inside again—but that's not happening now. Still, I know things about their structure and their communication. I'd appreciate it if you'd stress that to whoever holds my future in their hands."

The look he gave her was full of sympathy. "I promise you I will."

She swallowed the lump in her throat. There was nothing more she could do, nothing more she could ask for. But it was hard not to know, hard to imagine everything she'd done hadn't been enough. She put her hand over her belly automatically, wanting to protect her baby. Wanting the best for him or her.

Her cell phone buzzed against her leg, startling her. She fished it from her pocket and looked at the display. Then she looked up at Ian as she answered in the Qu'rimi dialect. He watched her carefully, but she focused on the call, her heart pounding at the voice on the other end.

"You must come today," Hassan Mustafa said. "They

are moving the hostages tonight."

"Do you know where they are?"

"Yes. You must come. And bring my money."

"Tell me where they are and I'll make sure you get the money. There's no time to waste."

He snorted. "I am no fool, Light of Zaran. You will come to the café in three hours. And you will have my money."

The line went dead.

TWENTY-TWO

"IT'S A HIGH-TRAFFIC AREA IN broad daylight," Emily said. "Nothing's going to happen."

Ryan stood with arms folded over his wide chest, his expression hard and angry. Nick didn't look much better. The rest of the guys were in full mission-planning mode, so they weren't nearly as pissed off as her lover and her sister's fiancé. After Mustafa called, she and Ian had sent for HOT so they could start to prepare for the operation to rescue the hostages. They needed to be ready to go when she got the location out of her contact. They most likely wouldn't go until it was dark, but they would get into position long before then. As soon as the time was right, they'd descend on the Freedom Force's hideout and liberate the hostages.

Emily's heart fluttered with excitement and apprehension. Soon, if all went well, they'd know where Linda Cooper and her colleagues were. And Linda would be reunited with her husband before another day passed.

"I don't like it," Ryan said. "He knows we're planning something, and he threw a curveball to disrupt those plans."

"Damn straight," Nick said. "He wants the money. He doesn't give a damn what happens to the hostages."

Emily rolled her eyes. "Yeah, I think we can all agree that Hassan Mustafa doesn't care about the hostages. That doesn't mean he's lying. He wants the money. The Freedom Force is moving the hostages tonight, which means no money for him. I think it's obvious what's at stake here."

"We have no choice," Matt said. "This is the mission, and this is what we're dealing with. Emily's the contact. But she doesn't have to go without backup."

Ian leaned against the wall in one corner of the room, arms crossed, surveying everyone with interest. "If Emily doesn't go to that meeting, you guys can kiss those hostages good-bye. Is that what you want?"

Ryan whirled on him. "What I want is Emily safe. Excuse me for not wanting the woman carrying my child to go to a fucking meeting with a greedy asshole who thinks it's okay to blow up women and children for a cause."

"He's not blowing anyone up," Ian said. "Not today. He wants the money. I'm not sure why this is so hard for you to comprehend. Must be an Army thing. I've always heard you don't have to be too bright to join the Army, but I never realized how true it was until today."

"You motherfucker," Ryan growled, taking a step toward where Ian stood.

Nick reached up and grabbed him by the collar, stopping his forward motion.

"At ease, you assholes," Matt said, his voice raised, each word firing into the air like a bullet. "Now's not the time for this shit."

Ryan shrugged off Nick's hand and stood there looking like he could chew steel for breakfast. Emily wanted to go over and touch his arm, assure him it would be all right. But she also wanted to smack him. He'd said he wouldn't interfere, and yet he'd done nothing except try to stop her from meeting with Mustafa from the minute he'd walked into this room.

He didn't trust her to do the job she'd come here to do, and it infuriated her. He insisted on treating her like she was the same broken creature she'd been when HOT had found her in the terrorist camp near Ras al-Dura. She wasn't that person any longer. She hadn't been for a long time, and he was a big part of the reason. He'd listened to her and given her encouragement—but clearly that encouragement only went so far as doing what he thought she should be doing. So long as she'd been a college student grappling with classes and dating, he'd been satisfied.

He didn't understand that this was who she really was. That she was tough and capable and that she wanted to be useful in the way he was useful. She *was* tough, even if she sometimes got scared. Who didn't get scared from time to time? But that didn't make her a coward. She was finally realizing that.

Ian looked at his watch. "We've got two hours. I suggest you stop arguing and get down to planning, or this entire op is going to hell faster than a preacher stealing from the collection plate. I'd rather not have to tell my boss that HOT is one big fucking failure. And I'm sure every one of you jerks would rather dance naked in a minefield than tell Mendez you couldn't get your shit together and rescue the people you came here to save."

"We aren't leaving without those hostages," Matt said tightly. "You worry about the money and let us take care of the rest."

"I'd love to… but your boys here can't seem to get past the idea that Emily's involved. You try sending someone else in there, Mustafa could run and those hostages will be on the nightly news by tomorrow night. It has to be Emily. He trusts her."

Ian had other operatives, sure, but none of them had the singular experience of having been inside the Freedom Force. That was what set her apart and what made Mustafa talk to her more than he had anyone else that Ian had ever sent. She knew the proper forms of address and modes of conduct, the way to massage his ego while still getting what she wanted out of him. She wasn't certain it was a matter of trust so much as comfortable familiarity.

She glanced at Ryan. He was watching her with a look of such anguish on his face that her heart cracked just a little bit.

"It's daylight," she said again. "It'll be safe. I'll be in and out."

If he'd had a worst nightmare, this would be it. Ryan watched Emily sitting with Ian Black and counting money before they stuffed the five bundles of one thousand hundred-dollar bills into a canvas messenger bag. She was about to walk out of here with that bag, out into the hot, dusty street where she'd make her way to the café near the market again.

Yeah, it was daylight and they could see everyone coming and going from the place, but he still didn't like it. Emily, the woman he'd made love to last night, the woman who rocked his world and had his baby in her belly, was about to don a full abaya and slip out to meet a terrorist while carrying enough money to choke a horse.

When she finished counting the money, she looked up and caught his gaze. He jerked his chin toward the door. He wasn't sure she'd go, but she stood and made her way toward it. When she slipped out, he went behind a few seconds later. The flash of her blond hair disappeared up the stairs and he followed, taking them two at a time until he hit the landing and found her standing at her bedroom door. She held it open and he went over and stepped inside, shutting the door behind him. She'd gone over to sit on the bed.

The bed they'd done so many amazing things together in last night.

"I know you're upset," she said, spreading her hands on her legs. "But I've told you from the beginning that I had a job to do."

He wanted to say that it was too dangerous, but the words stuck in his throat. How many times had he said them already?

"It's half a million in cash. He wants the money. He won't care who delivers it. It doesn't have to be you."

She snorted. "He's paranoid. Of course he cares who delivers it. If one of you shows up, looking like you do—all big and muscular and meaner than a rattlesnake—he's going to slip away like he was never there. I have to be there, and I have to be sitting in the same place I always sit—or as near to it as possible if the table's taken. You'll be outside, Ryan. If something happens, you'll bust in and get me out."

Yeah, he damn well would. No matter what the cost to himself.

She stood and came over to him, tilted her head up to look at him. "I'm not happy with you right now, but I understand why you want to stop me. What I need you to realize is that you can't. And that you trust I'm the right person for this job. I'm the only one with the skills and knowledge, Ryan."

Fuck. "I trust you. It's not about that. It's about this fucking place, about everything that could go wrong out there. About our baby, our future."

"I know this is about our future—why do you think it's so important to me? I have to prove myself, prove I'm an asset and not a security risk. If I can't do that—" She swallowed, her brown eyes glistening. "I can't let my mistakes color this child's life."

"You don't know that they will. He'll have the same opportunities as anyone."

She shook her head. "You really don't understand what it's like to be me. I've told you how important this is to me, Ryan. I won't sit this one out to make you feel better. You need to get over it and focus on the mission."

He reeled as if she'd slapped him. "I am focused."

"You aren't. You're as scattered as a cat chasing ten mice. You need to snap out of it."

He growled. And then he grasped her by the upper arms and dragged her in close. "I'm focused, honey. Focused on you and our child. I'll be on your ass out there, and if that fucker so much as looks at you cross-eyed, I'm coming in. I protect what's mine, Emily—and you're mine. I don't care what the fuck you think about us getting married or any half-assed ideas you have about being a single mother. It's not going down that way. You're marrying me, even if I have to take you bound and gagged to the preacher. And don't think I won't do it, either. Brandy will fucking help me. Victoria won't say a word."

Her eyes were like saucers, but she wasn't struggling to get away. And then her gaze dropped to his mouth, and he shuddered with the force of his need for her. Right now. Every day. He needed her in his life. In his bed.

He *needed* her. Ryan blinked with the realization that he'd somehow come to need a specific person in his life. How had it happened? Did that mean he loved her?

Holy shit, that's exactly what it meant. For months now, she'd been a part of his life, a comfortable part that he took for granted like a television or a cell phone. He'd expected her to always be there, and when she hadn't been, he'd felt betrayed. Lost. He'd spent two months quietly stewing about the fact that she'd left him.

And now she was here, in his arms, and she was about to leave him again. It terrified him.

Her brow pleated in concern, and he knew his expression must have changed pretty dramatically. "You okay, Ry?"

"Yeah," he said past the huge knot in his throat. He wrapped his arms around her and held her close. She came willingly, slipping her arms around his waist and laying her head over his heart. She was small and soft, and he lifted his hand to stroke her hair. He wanted to tell her what he felt, what he'd realized.

But a part of him held back. If he told her now, would he throw her off her game with Mustafa? Would she be distracted?

"I like that you care," she said, her voice muffled against his chest. "Maybe I'll marry you after all."

He snorted. "Already told you there's no choice."

"There's always a choice."

"Not this time, honey."

She pushed away until she could look into his eyes. "I think we have a lot to talk about."

"Yeah, I think we do."

Someone pounded on the door and Emily flinched. But she didn't take her eyes from his.

"Showtime," she whispered.

"Hey, you two in there?" Fiddler shouted. "We've got to get moving."

"Coming," Ryan answered. But not before he kissed Emily. He lowered his head and captured her mouth. She melted into him, her body pliant and soft, her mouth responsive and sweet.

It was a hot, desperate kiss filled with too many emotions to name. And it was over all too soon. Emily broke away first, her fingers curling into his shirt as she pushed him back.

"We have to go, Ry. Time to find Linda Cooper and her colleagues."

There was a ball of despair sitting in his gut. "As soon as this is over, we're talking. About everything and anything."

She smiled. "I know. I can't wait."

TWENTY-THREE

MENDEZ SAT AT HIS DESK, studying the files an aide had brought, when his secure phone rang. He whipped it up with a clipped "Mendez."

"Hello, John." It was Samantha Spencer's voice. He would know that soft, sultry tone anywhere, even if he rarely heard it. A mild electrical current sizzled through him at the sound. It was pleasant, not overwhelming, and maybe even somewhat fascinating.

"Sam. How did you get this number?"

She laughed. "Don't ask, don't tell. Suffice it to say I got it."

The secure phone on his desk was known to only a few people. Very few. When it rang, he knew it was important. Perhaps even critical to the safety of the world.

But this was Sam, and she didn't sound as if she had a pressing issue for him.

"What do you need from me?"

This time her laugh sent a prickle of arousal down his spine, tingling into his balls.

"Oh, Johnny. If we had but world enough and time."

She cleared her throat. "But no, this is about your situation in Acamar."

His senses went on high alert. He hadn't been told she was on this mission in any capacity, but apparently she was. And she definitely had his attention now.

"What do you have?"

"Nothing much, just some buzz—and it might not mean a thing. You know there's a woman in charge now? Raja?"

"Yes." He shouldn't be surprised that Sam knew, but he was. "Do you have something on her?"

"Not exactly, but we've been listening for her name. It came up twice today… and so did Emily bin Yusuf's."

"What about Emily?"

"Raja wants to meet Emily."

Fuck. "Any idea why?"

"No, not really. But I thought you should know."

"I appreciate the tip." He wasn't certain what it meant, but there was no such thing as a useless piece of information in his world. Everything had a meaning—you just had to find it.

"I knew you would… If you want to thank me in person, you can come to the bar tomorrow night. I'll be there."

"With your date?"

"Not this time, Johnny. It'll just be me… and you."

Emily slipped the abaya over her clothing. The beauty of this particular garment was that it covered the messenger bag she'd draped crossways over her shoulder. It wasn't everyday she walked around with a half a million in one-hundred-dollar bills strapped to her body. That was five thousand bills, each weighing a gram. Or approximately eleven pounds total.

It seemed like half a million dollars should weigh more, but it didn't. It was like picking up a hand weight in the gym, or a Thanksgiving turkey for a small gathering. How many turkeys could she buy with this much dough anyway?

It wasn't even all that bulky. Each stack of one thousand bills was 4.3 inches thick.

Ryan held a small square that looked like one of those breath strips that typically came in a hard plastic package. When she had the abaya situated and she'd fixed the hijab over her hair, he came over and took her arm, lifting it up and pushing the sleeve of the abaya back.

"A little present from HOT," he said, pressing the square to her skin. It immediately stuck to her, fading as he rubbed it on.

"What is that?"

"A bio-tracker."

She looked at the spot where he'd put the tracker. She couldn't even tell it was there anymore. "Nice stuff if you can get it, 007."

Ryan grinned. "HOT is the best of the best. Of course we have all the cool toys."

Billy Blake looked up from where he hunkered over his laptop. "Got your signal loud and clear."

Emily sighed as she looked at Ryan again. "I'm only

going to the café, you guys. You'll have a visual on me. This thing might just be overkill."

She held her arm up and studied the spot. Not a trace of the bio-tracker was there. Knowing HOT, it was experimental technology—and probably pretty expensive at that. She didn't think Mendez would appreciate them using up assets on her.

"Maybe, but it makes me feel better knowing you're wearing it."

Tenderness flooded her. Oh, this man made her insides flutter. And when she thought of that little speech he'd made about marrying her no matter what?

Yeah, total melted-panty moment. She'd been mad and turned on all at once. And she'd been about to tell him off, except that he'd suddenly gotten this look like he was lost in a vast forest and couldn't remember how to find his way out again. She'd wanted to ask him about that look, but he'd dragged her into his arms and she'd loved being next to him so much that she'd gone without question.

She wished now that she'd asked, because they'd run out of time when Fiddler interrupted. Ryan had said they would talk, but she didn't know when that would be now. After she got the hostages' location from Mustafa, HOT was going to work. What if they went after the hostages immediately? She very likely wouldn't see Ryan again until they were Stateside.

That thought made her shudder. There was something about knowing he might not be here tonight that didn't feel right.

"We ready?" Nick asked, strolling into the room.

Nick, Ryan, Iceman, and Fiddler were going with her for this meeting. Billy would monitor her conversation and location from the compound while the other guys prepared for the mission to rescue the hostages. She prayed that Mustafa delivered so they could do their jobs. So Linda Cooper could be reunited with her husband in Italy.

"I'm ready," Emily said.

"Let's roll," Iceman replied, swinging the strap of his assault rifle over his shoulder. The others were similarly armed. No half measures for them today. They wore Arab clothing, including the *kaffiyeh* with black *igal* cords to hold the head covering in place—but they also carried weapons openly, which wasn't unusual for Acamar or Qu'rim these days. There was always fighting going on in the desert and the border areas. Before long, if it wasn't contained in Qu'rim, it would reach all the way to Al-Izir. In fact, the presence of the Freedom Force in the city was already an ominous sign.

"Wait a minute," Ryan said with a growl before turning back to Emily. "Your comm link still working?"

Emily touched the mic hidden in her clothing. "You hear me?"

"Loud and clear. You?"

She'd heard his voice being delivered in her ear as if he were standing right there and talking into it. "I hear you."

"We've been over it a hundred times already," Iceman grumbled. "Her shit works. Your shit works. All our shit works. Let's go and find out where those hostages are. I want to get home to Grace by the weekend, so let's stop talking and get moving."

"We'll be here waiting for your signal," Matt said as they started for the street. "As soon as you can get us the location, we'll start working on an extraction plan."

When they reached the exterior door, Iceman and Nick went out first. She waited with Ryan until she could step out. He would follow when she'd been gone for thirty seconds.

He caught her hand and squeezed. "You be careful out there, honey. I need you to come back in one piece."

His words warmed her. "Same here, Ry. This baby needs two parents in his life."

"Yeah, I…"

Her heart thumped. "What, Ryan?"

His smile got her right in the pit of her stomach. "It can wait. You need to think about this meeting and Mustafa."

She knew she did, and yet he was always front and center in her mind. Especially now. She lifted on tiptoe and pressed her lips to his. Then she slipped out the door and started the long walk to the market.

Mustafa wasn't there when she arrived, but then she hadn't expected him to be. The café was crowded this afternoon with men and women—though mostly men—having the strong, sweet Arab coffee flavored with cardamom that they preferred.

Acamar hadn't gone so far as to prohibit men and women from frequenting the same establishments yet, but she feared it was coming if the Freedom Force had their way. She took a table in the back, not the usual one she sat at, but close to it, and waited.

She had the proprietor bring her water and coffee even though she knew she couldn't drink the coffee now that she was pregnant. She sipped the water and let her gaze slide over the café and the market. It was crowded too, with people bargaining for vegetables, meats, and spices. There was a rug dealer hawking his wares, beautiful handwoven carpets made by the women of Acamarian villages. She'd bought one of those rugs, a small one, for her room when she first arrived two months ago.

There was also a copper seller whose hand-hammered pots would bring a fortune in a specialty store in a US mall, but here were perfectly ordinary and used by women as daily cooking vessels and not showpieces to hang over a kitchen island.

Emily scanned the area, seeking her HOT boys. She wouldn't find them, but she knew they were there. She touched her mic while bending her head to blow on her coffee.

"Are you in position yet?"

"I can see you at the table in the back," Ryan said. "You're talking to your coffee."

She wanted to laugh but she somehow managed to keep a straight face. "No, I'm talking to you."

"Sure you are, honey."

"Ry…? Can the others hear us?" She'd only talked to him during the setup, so she wasn't sure. Maybe they could say a few things now while they were waiting.

"Oh yeah."

"Oh… too bad."

He snorted. "Yeah."

"Jesus, enough with the flirting," Nick grumbled.

"She's practically my baby sister. It's creepy to listen in."

"Better get used to it, Brandy," Ryan said. "Because when we return Stateside, I'm marrying her. That'll make us brothers or something. Won't family picnics be a blast?"

Nick snorted. "Great, now I'll have to hang out with you in our off time too. Just what I wanted."

Emily couldn't help but smile. These guys were already close, all of them, but they had to razz each other anyway. Neither one of them was going to be upset about family picnics or whatever it was they ended up doing together.

Wait… did that mean she was seriously going to marry him? Yeah, maybe it did. Maybe it would be okay after all. If Mustafa would just show up and give them the coordinates, then HOT could get to rescuing the hostages. And maybe that would be enough for Ian's contacts to clear her name.

A tall man clad in desert robes made his way toward the café, and her insides squeezed tight. Hassan Mustafa walked with purpose, like always. And why wouldn't he? If everything went well, he'd be leaving here with enough money to disappear into a part of the world where the Freedom Force couldn't find him. It wouldn't be enough for an American, but for a Qu'rimi man who'd lived a life of hardship and deprivation, it was enough to live like a king in the right location.

He glanced around before entering the café. Carefully, he made his way to her table and sat down. The proprietor was there immediately with a coffee. When he walked away, Mustafa's dark eyes bored into her.

"Do you have it?"

"Yes. Do you?"

His gaze sharpened for a second before settling back into its usual gleam of mild irritation. "Yes."

"Then tell me where to find them, and you'll get your package."

He followed her hand as she ran it over the lump beneath her robe. He sat back and took a sip of the coffee. "How do I know what that is?"

"You don't. And I don't know that what you're about to tell me will be the truth."

He leaned forward suddenly and her heartbeat kicked up. "I have risked my life to get this information," he spat out. "I have no reason to lie."

"That's good," she told him coolly. "Because if what you tell me is false, you will be hunted down and dealt with. It won't be pretty, I promise you that."

He sneered. "You will not find me once we are done here today. This is the end."

"You aren't inspiring my confidence."

There was a disturbance of some sort in the market then, and her gaze went to it the same as his did. She couldn't tell what the issue was, but her heart thumped at the chaos of bodies and yelling. Her first instinct was to run, but this wasn't a bomb or anything. It was some sort of disagreement in the market, no doubt.

Mustafa turned to look at her again—and then he shot to his feet and she gasped. She started to tell him to sit back down, that they weren't done yet, but he wasn't looking at her at all. He was looking with wide eyes behind her. He started to fumble for his weapon, and Emily bolted up, whirling.

Two men with balaclavas over their faces rushed toward her and Mustafa. "Ryan," she screamed as the men raised their weapons.

But whether he heard her or not, she didn't know. A hot blast came from one of the guns at that moment, and people screamed. Tables scraped and turned over, and someone grabbed her and yanked her out of the way. She thought maybe it was Ryan, but when she turned, a dark hood slipped over her head. She was lifted, kicking and screaming, and thrown over a hard shoulder.

It knocked the breath out of her, made her choke. *My baby!* Her assailant's shoulder had jammed into her abdomen, crashing right into where her precious tiny baby was living and growing. If something happened to her baby…

Emily moaned the word *no*, fighting for consciousness, gripping the man's clothing and willing herself to let go and punch him. But the hood was stifling and breathing was difficult. Her limbs wouldn't move. Her head bounced against his back as he ran. It was everything she could do to pull in air.

And then suddenly she couldn't.

TWENTY-FOUR

"WHAT THE FUCK JUST HAPPENED?" Ryan roared at the sound of a gunshot. He sprinted for the café along with Ice and Brandy. They'd been in the market, watching and listening. When an old lady started yelling at a vendor, Ryan had only half paid attention. Then a young man jumped into the fray, a market stall of vegetables became a food fight, and the crowd started to grumble and take sides.

Of course it had been meant as a distraction. He knew that now. They all did.

Fiddler was supposed to be watching the rear of the building in which the café was housed, but he hadn't sounded an alarm. Since the café was in the middle of a busy market, there were people coming and going from everywhere. Probably there'd been nothing unusual in anything he'd seen.

"I have no fucking idea," came Fiddler's growled reply in response. "They must have been inside the building already."

Ryan's heart beat double time as he ran. He burst into

the café, gun aloft. The people still there screamed anew, lifting hands over heads. A body lay on the floor, blood pooling around him in a steady stream.

It was Hassan Mustafa. Ryan bent to take his pulse, but there was none. He'd been shot in the chest at point-blank range. That much was clear from the blood spatter on the walls and floor. The proprietor chattered in Arabic while wringing his hands. There was a door on one wall that stood open, and Ryan rushed toward it. It led into a shop filled with furniture and household goods. Overhead, copper pans banged together as if someone had rushed through only recently and hit them all on the way.

"Emily," he said into the mic. "Where are you? Can you hear me? Emily!"

The shopkeeper stood with hands over his head, pointing the way toward the back of the shop. Ryan stalked down the narrow path, sweeping the gun right and left, hoping beyond hope to find Emily back there.

"Anything?" Brandy said.

"Nothing here," Iceman replied.

"Nothing," Fiddler added.

Fear and fury swirled in Ryan's belly. "Not yet. But we'll find her. Jesus, we have to find her."

"We've got the bio-tracker—don't forget that. We'll get her back."

He hadn't forgotten, but if he stopped searching now, if he walked away and went back to Black's compound without turning over every stone there, he feared something would happen to her before they could find her. Tracker or not, he was scared for her. For his woman. His baby.

He swept all the way to the back of the shop and then

burst through the rear door. There was nothing but a street there, and it was packed with people and cars. He scanned the area, looking for Emily, for anything familiar or out of place, then whirled and went back inside. When he found a stairwell, he kicked in the door and started up the stairs.

But there was nothing up there except living quarters, presumably for the shopkeeper. The first room was empty except for a couple of chairs, a rug, and a television. There was another with an open door, and Ryan moved toward it. The room contained a bed and little else. There were no closets. He lowered the gun and made his way down the stairs again.

He met his team at the front of the shop. None of them had Emily. And they didn't look happy.

"We have to get back to the compound," Ice said. "Kid's got data on the tracker."

His heart hurt. His soul hurt. Everything hurt. Full-blown panic threatened to blossom in his chest and take him to his knees. "Where is she?"

"Moving away from the market."

Ryan hefted his weapon. "We need to go after her. Right fucking now."

Brandy put a hand on his arm. "They're moving too fast. They're in a car and we're on foot."

"The streets are logjammed with traffic. We can catch them."

Ice shook his head. "They're moving steadily. Kid says they'll hit the outskirts in five minutes. If we're lucky, they'll lead us to the hostages."

Ryan blinked. Rage swelled in his gut, his throat. "Wait a minute… You want to let them take her away so we can find out where the hostages are? What if they don't waste any time before they kill her, huh? What then, ass-hole?"

Ice got up in his face, his expression filled with fury. "No one wants Emily hurt. *No one*. It's a fucking insult for you to suggest any of us want to *use* her to lead us to the hostages. If it turns out that way, then maybe we can salvage this mission. But nobody wanted it to happen like this."

He knew better, he really did, but knowing they'd lost her right out from under their noses made him question everything. Were they slipping? Every team had a failure, and while he'd thought they'd had theirs when two members died during an operation a couple of years ago, maybe they were headed for another.

And this time it involved Emily.

No.

"They want her alive," Fiddler said. "They killed Mustafa on the spot."

"We're wasting time," Brandy ground out. "Let's get back to HQ so we can find Emily and free those hostages."

Ryan couldn't do anything but go mutely with them. They took off at a jog, making their way back to Black's compound in about ten minutes. Grim faces greeted them as they entered the room where HOT had set up their command center. Ian Black was there, but he didn't say anything for a change.

"We've still got her," Kid said as they walked in. "They're on the highway, moving out of the city."

Matt had a map spread out on a table. "Looks like they're heading for the border."

"Then what are we waiting for?" Ryan asked. "Let's go."

Matt looked up. "We can't go yet, Flash."

"Why the fuck not?"

"Mendez's orders."

Emily was aware of movement beneath her. Tires on sand. Her breath was hot on her face, which meant she was still wearing the hood—but it wasn't tight. She could breathe, though the smells coming from the vehicle almost made her wish she couldn't.

Unwashed, sweaty bodies and stale cigarette smoke. The two men in the café had definitely been Freedom Force, but there were probably others now. Mustafa had recognized them—and been terrified. With good reason, considering he'd been betraying them.

They must have figured it out and followed him. His life was forfeit now. And maybe hers as well, especially when they figured out who she was. Light of Zaran. The wife of one of their commanders, a woman who had gone missing the night he died—a night in which an American Special Ops team had infiltrated the camp at Ras al-Dura. Maybe they would blame her for it.

She could tell by the lack of weight on her ankle that her holster was empty. They'd removed the gun. Her knives were gone too.

One of the men said something, and she focused on his voice. She didn't recognize it, but she could understand what he said. Perhaps he didn't know that yet—or perhaps he didn't care.

It didn't matter much anyway because he didn't say anything important. A grumble that he was nearly out of cigarettes. Another man answered, telling him they'd be back at the camp soon.

She wished she knew which camp. Her heart raced and her belly ached. She put a hand over her middle and held it there, praying her baby was okay. If she lost this child, what if she never got pregnant again? What if this was her only chance?

She squeezed her eyes shut and prayed harder. Soon the vehicle slowed. A few moments later, it stopped and the doors were flung open. She could tell by the wash of desert air that rolled inside. It was hot, which meant it was still daylight. That was good because she had no idea how long she'd been passed out.

But if it was still day, that meant she hadn't been out too long and they hadn't driven far. Twenty or thirty miles maybe. She hoped like hell that bio-tracker thing Ryan had put on her worked.

Her chest ached at the thought of him. He would be blaming himself for this. The fact he hadn't gotten there in time, hadn't stopped these men from taking her, would be killing him. He'd told her she would be safe, and she knew she would be.

She *believed* she would be. She had to believe it, or she'd go crazy.

Rough hands grabbed her and jerked her up. The strap from the messenger bag tightened as she stood, the familiar weight of the money still there. That was a surprise considering they'd searched her enough to take her weapon. She stumbled and reached out to break her fall, her hands colliding with cloth. Whoever it was cursed at her and shoved her back. She fell onto her butt and then turned on her knees and managed to get up again while he yelled obscenities at her. She didn't dare take the sack off her head, even though she could because her hands were free.

A hard hand gripped her by the elbow and guided her down from the vehicle.

Someone grabbed the edge of the sack and ripped it up and off. Emily blinked against the bright daylight, lifting her hands to shield her eyes.

"What are you doing, idiot?" someone yelled. "I told you not to harm the woman."

"She is not harmed, Your Excellency."

"You touch her again and you die." The voice was closer now. It was a hard male voice that tickled her memory. She slid her hand from her eyes slowly, blinking. The desert sun was harsh, but it was sinking into the sky now and the light was more golden than white.

A man stood before her in long white robes, the kaffiyeh on his head fluttering in a breeze that chose that particular moment to blow. When she focused on him fully, he touched his head and his heart before bowing low. The men around her did the same as if their movements were somehow tied to his.

What the ... ?

Emily's mouth dropped open, but nothing came out. She knew this man. Malik ibn Essa, a junior lieutenant who'd been under Zaran's command. When he spoke again, a fresh chill wrapped around her heart and squeezed it with icy fingers.

"Light of Zaran, we are glad you have come home to us."

TWENTY-FIVE

THE WAITING WAS THE WORST PART. Ryan jumped to his feet and resumed his circuit of the room. He'd been up and down probably ten times, but he couldn't sit still. His team—and Echo Squad—sat around the room, waiting much more patiently than he did.

Ian Black had left a while ago. Ryan was glad, because he didn't want to look at the man's face. It was Black's fault Emily was here, Black's fault she'd been meeting with Mustafa in the first place. Looking at him only made Ryan want to kill him. Something of which he was sure Mendez would not approve.

He knew what they were waiting for. Mendez had sent a drone with thermal imaging capabilities and an advanced radar system that would give them a readout on the technical specifications of the place where Emily was being held. They needed to know that information if they were going to break in.

And they needed confirmation that the hostages were there. Thermal imaging would be able to detect the bodies and pinpoint with one hundred percent accuracy how many men and women there were. For the hostages, it should be five women and eight men. Of course there would be others in the camp, but it was likely the hostages were all together. Or separated by sex, which would still help HOT confirm their presence.

The information on Emily's bio-tracker hadn't changed. It was functioning, which meant she was still alive. That didn't make it any easier on him. Her vital signs weren't ideal. Her blood pressure was up and her heart rate was faster than it should be.

That was fear. But nothing had changed recently, which meant her situation hadn't changed. They weren't torturing her—but for how long would that last?

He hated to think what they would do to her once they got whatever it was they wanted. He simply didn't believe anyone in the Freedom Force was naïve enough to think she was still on their side. Her husband was dead and she'd been gone for months. Now she showed up in a café with half a million dollars and a meeting with a man they'd killed rather than take with them.

Yeah, none of that was good.

Fuck, why hadn't he told her he loved her? Why had he thought she didn't need to hear it before she went to meet Mustafa? Emily was bright and capable. She wouldn't have been distracted by his revelation. She would have done the job she was supposed to do—and they'd probably still be in the same situation. Whoever had taken her knew to expect she'd have backup. They'd made sure to stage a physical distraction that made it difficult for the team to maneuver the crowd as quickly as they otherwise would.

"Incoming message," Kid said, and Ryan spun and

walked over to where everyone gathered. Kid turned the combat-hardened laptop so everyone could see it and then hit a button. Colonel Mendez appeared on-screen.

"Good evening, gentlemen," he said, even though it was morning in DC. "We have all the information we need. The hostages are located approximately thirty miles southeast of Al-Izir, quite close to the Lost City where they were taken. There's a small village there—Kharat— and Emily's signal is coming from a compound on the western edge. She's being held in a separate room from the hostages, that much we can see, though that information could change by the time you get there. The drone will make another pass in an hour, and the information will be sent directly to you. The schematic for the buildings is being sent now. Sergeant Blake will make sure it's loaded onto your Hawkeye prototypes for real-time targeting." Mendez looked down at his watch, back up again. "This is your go-order, men. Find our fellow Americans and bring them home safely."

"Yes, sir!" everyone said at once.

The call ended and they rocketed into motion.

Malik ushered her inside, talking like they were old friends who had accidentally bumped into each other at the store one day. He was chatty, polite, but her pulse hammered nevertheless. She didn't trust him.

She almost laughed at that thought. *Of course* she

didn't fucking trust him! He was a terrorist. He also wasn't an idiot, which made the fact he was treating her like she'd just returned home after a long trip away very odd and a little frightening. Okay, a lot frightening.

Emily darted her gaze around the compound at every step, looking for signs of the hostages, for ways to escape, for anything that sparked a thought about why she was here and what they wanted from her.

She still had the money on her body, so they hadn't searched her. But there was no feedback in her earpiece, no sound of any kind, and she wondered if the link was broken or if HOT was just silent. She prayed they were out there. Coming for her.

Malik indicated a chair at a table and she sat, her body a little stiff from the ride on the floor of the van and the way she'd been thrown around. He went and poured some water from a pitcher and returned to give it to her.

She took it, but then she set it down, her mouth dry but her mind running through the possibilities of being drugged or poisoned.

Malik laughed and went over to pour a glass for himself. Then he drank it.

She reached for hers and took a sip. Tasted like water. She sipped again, carefully, waiting for signs of poison.

There were none.

"So tell me," Malik said breezily, coming to take a seat opposite her, "how did you come to be in Acamar?"

Such a strange conversation. Emily cleared her throat. She was sweating beneath the abaya, but she couldn't take it off. Not here where to do so would be considered vulgar by the men.

"Ian Black made me an offer I couldn't refuse." No

sense in lying about it. He knew she wasn't here as a tour-
ist, and Black had had dealings with the Freedom Force in
the past. He'd told her that he'd actually stopped HOT
from killing Zaran once. She'd found that amazing, but
then Ian's agenda was something she'd never understand
as long as she lived. He didn't seem to have a side sometimes, but she was positive his side was the same as
HOT's, even if he got there a different way.

"Ah, Mr. Black. Yes, he is familiar to me. I believe he
sold us some rifles not so long ago."

"That's Ian."

"Why did you not come to us, Light of Zaran? Your
disappearance was most distressing, especially after the
Americans invaded our camp."

She took another sip of water. "I, uh, I wasn't certain
I would be welcome. Zaran was dead, after all."

He made a sad face. It was almost comical since she
suspected he wasn't sad at all. Zaran's death would have
elevated him. Indeed, it must have since he'd been addressed like someone of importance earlier.

"Yes, may Allah bless our lost brother... But you
would have been taken care of, as the widow of a dead
hero should be."

She wanted to shiver. She managed not to. "I was
captured by the Americans. And since I am one, they took
me back to America. They believed I had knowledge they
could use."

"But you had none, because you are not a warrior for
the cause."

"That's right. I know you—many of you—but not
your true selves, or where you are from. That's what they
wanted. I had nothing to give them."

Malik smiled. "No, you wouldn't have. This is good… Now tell me about Hassan Mustafa and the money you are carrying."

A jolt of fear went through her, but she managed not to let it show. Or so she hoped anyway. His expression didn't change as he watched her. She got the impression of a cat hunkering in the shadows, waiting for the mouse to move.

"Ian was paying him for information."

"What kind of information?"

Emily clenched her fists in her lap and took a deep breath. This was ridiculous and she knew it. He wasn't being friendly. Or solicitous. He had a purpose, and when he was done with her, he'd probably kill her himself.

"Why don't you ask Mustafa?"

He leaned back in his chair and shrugged. "Alas, this is not possible. He is dead."

Another jolt of fear went through her. And anger as well. She hadn't necessarily liked or disliked Mustafa, but he was a person she'd spent time with. She could still see his dark eyes, the way he tucked his pipe between his lips—and the fear earlier today when he'd seen the men in the café. The gunshot she'd heard—it made sense now.

"I'm sorry to hear that," she said and meant it.

"He was a traitor. He did not believe in the cause."

She didn't say anything.

"Do you believe in the cause, Light of Zaran?"

"I believe in freedom from oppression for everyone." It was a neutral answer, but it was also a correct answer.

The gleam in his eyes said he understood as much. He got to his feet then and looked down at her. "You may stay in this room. There will be food brought. Eat it or don't.

Your choice."

"Why did you bring me here?" she asked as he whirled and stalked to the door.

He stopped with his hand on the handle. "You will find out when the time is right. Peace, Light of Zaran."

She watched as the door closed behind him—but then it opened again and she jumped as he stuck his head back inside.

"Oh, I meant to tell you that your microphones and listening devices have been neutralized. *Inshallah.*"

This time when the door closed, it stayed closed. Emily made herself breathe in and out very slowly, very carefully. She had no link to HOT. No way to talk to Ryan. She didn't need that so long as the bio-tracker he'd put on her arm was working.

But she had no idea if it was. Or if HOT would ever find her again.

TWENTY-SIX

"FLASH, REPORT."

"In position," Ryan said.

Beside him, Fiddler and Iceman gave the same answer in response to the question. They'd arrived twenty minutes ago. First, they'd taken trucks out into the desert as far as they could go, and then they'd crossed on foot, silent and determined, until they came within sight of the village.

There were lights on in the town, but they didn't want to walk into the middle of it. The Freedom Force would know they were there within moments if they did. No; instead, they took a course that brought them to the western edge and the compound that intel had identified.

The schematic for the facility appeared in their Hawkeye night vision goggles. These NVGs were new and wicked cool. Not only did they allow for advanced vision in the dark, but they were capable of thermal imaging and had an onboard targeting system that worked like a video game to enable the person wearing them to walk into any structure as if they knew where they were going.

Every man wore them, and every single one could bust into that compound and know where he was immediately.

They'd split up when they left the trucks, but now they were converging again, getting ready to storm the facility. Two men would target the generator while the others worked on neutralizing the opposition. There were ten men with weapons prowling around the compound. There was a woman in a room by herself, and another room on the lower level with thirteen people inside.

Ryan and his companions were going for the woman alone because that was Emily.

As soon as the team infiltrated the compound, Matt would give the order for the Blackhawks to come. They'd trucked in, but they'd fly out because they had no idea what the medical status of the prisoners was. And getting thirteen people—fourteen when you counted Emily—to run through the desert and make it to the trucks without anyone getting hurt or killed wasn't exactly a cakewalk.

"You hear that?" someone asked.

Ryan strained his ears against the night. And then he heard it—the sound of a helicopter's rotors beating the air.

"Fuck," Matt said.

"Is that our guys?" Ryan asked. "Because it's too fucking soon."

"No, it's not our guys."

The helicopter moved toward them, growing louder and louder in the night air. And then it came into view, a civilian craft that swung over the compound and began to descend in the courtyard.

"Fucking hell!" Big Mac said. "This is a problem. Everybody stand down until we get some info."

Emily didn't eat the food a man brought in and set down in front of her. He didn't say anything, and she didn't ask any questions. He was gone again quickly, and she jumped up once more and went to the window. She was on the second floor, and she thought if she could get the window open then maybe she could crawl out and drop.

But the window wouldn't open, and smashing something through it wasn't an option. Her captors would hear the sound and come immediately. Instead, she searched the room for something she could use as a weapon.

Other than throwing a chair at somebody, she couldn't find anything. This room hadn't been used for much probably, as there was nothing in it except chairs and a table.

She went back to the window, but it was dark out now and she could see nothing except a few village lights here and there. She stood for a long time—and then she heard a sound, a slight, rhythmic thumping.

And then it grew closer and she realized it was a helicopter. Her heart shot skyward. It was HOT! It was Ryan, come to get her. Relief flooded her even as she prepared to do battle with her bare hands. Soon her captors would realize they were being invaded, and they would come for her.

But as the helicopter drew closer and no one burst into her room, she began to realize she must be wrong. No one came—and there was no panic, no shouting inside the compound.

As she scanned the night sky, the helicopter appeared, its lights beaming down on the courtyard outside the window. It sank down like a bee kissing a flower, landing softly on the concrete pad she'd noticed earlier but ignored as unimportant.

The rotors slowed and the door opened. A man in a dark suit and a kaffiyeh emerged. And then a woman, dressed in a white abaya. Jewels sewn into the fabric caught the light and glittered as she walked. She was small, delicate. But her head was bowed, her hair covered in a hijab, and Emily couldn't see her face. A wife, no doubt. She was dressed too richly not to be.

But was it a wife she'd met before?

She chafed her arms as the chill in her heart seeped out into her limbs. The couple disappeared, and she turned away from the window. Soon voices echoed throughout the structure, and she knew the couple had come inside.

She went over to the door, straining to hear—and the voices grew louder. There were footsteps on the stairs, and she darted back to the other side of the table, instinctively wanting to keep it between her and whoever was coming.

The door opened, startling her even though she'd expected it. Malik walked in, and the man from the helicopter. He had narrow, beady eyes, and they watched her with undisguised dislike.

Then the woman entered, and Emily's breath caught. She was beautiful, delicate featured, and with a natural grace that most people didn't possess. She walked past the two men and came over to the table, making a great show of studying the chair for cleanliness before she sat.

She's in charge here. That thought hit Emily like a

dip into ice water. And then she had another thought: Raja.

This woman was Raja. There could be no other explanation. She traveled in a helicopter and she commanded these men. They deferred to her. It was obvious, and shocking as well in the patriarchal world of the Freedom Force.

"We finally meet, Light of Zaran," she said in a musical voice that sounded more appropriate for an opera singer than a terror leader. "I have looked forward to it."

"I-I'm not sure I can say the same. Who are you?" Because she didn't know for certain and because it didn't help to appear to know things before you were told. Not with these kind of people.

"You may call me Raja."

"Why did you want to meet me, Raja? I am no one." She spread her fingers, trying to look as meek as she could.

Raja laughed. The sound was like tiny bells tinkling. "Ah, but you have spent much time in Washington DC, and much time with the evil men who tried to bring down this organization when they kidnapped Al Ahmad. I am interested to know everything."

A fresh chill rolled down her spine then. This woman knew she'd been in DC? Knew about HOT? That was alarming in more ways than one.

"I have nothing to tell. I was not involved in any way. I was taken from the camp when my husband was killed, and returned to the United States. Beyond that, I know nothing."

Raja snorted. "Such a good liar, Emily Royal bin Yusuf. It took time to find you, but find you we did. And we watched you. I know who you are and who you care for." Raja's eyes grew black with fury then. If there had been a candle in the room, it would have guttered. "Someone is going to pay for taking our leader. I'm starting with you—but it won't end there, you can count on that."

She stood and stalked toward Emily. Emily didn't dare move, though Raja looked delicate and feminine rather than menacing.

"You will hand over the money beneath your abaya. And you will come with me. We have much to discuss—and it will not happen here."

"Where are you taking me?"

Raja's eyes flickered. "To Qu'rim."

Sweat sprang up on her palms, between her breasts. "What about the hostages? What do you plan to do with them?"

One of Raja's perfectly arched eyebrows lifted. "We will behead them, of course. Unless your government cooperates with our demands."

Emily's throat squeezed tight. Mustafa had been so wrong about this woman not approving of the hostages being taken. "They won't. America doesn't negotiate with terrorists."

Raja shrugged. "Then perhaps they might like to start." She jerked her head at the man in the suit. "Get the money and bring her. We're going."

"We're a go. Repeat, we're a go."

It had been ten minutes since the helicopter had land-ed. A tense ten minutes in which HOT waited to find out how many new people had arrived and where they were going. The heat signature said it was two men and one woman. The pilot remained onboard the craft, and a man and woman went inside. After a brief conference with an-other man, the three of them went up to where Emily was being held.

The prototype NVGs displayed the heat signatures of the people inside when switched to thermal mode. Emily hadn't moved since the three people entered her room, but the woman sat down while the men remained standing. A few seconds later, she stood.

That's when Matt gave the go order.

Ryan and his teammates shut off the thermal switch, enabling the real-time targeting feature for an accurate schematic of the building. They surged toward the com-pound in a wave, silent, deadly, and determined. The tan-gos hadn't been expecting anything apparently, because the door was easily breached. The lights switched out then as Cade Rodgers and his team reached the generator.

In other quadrants of the compound, men would be scaling the walls and kicking in windows. But Ryan, Fid-dler, and Iceman ran for the central building where every-one was being held. Their task was to go in the front door, up the stairs, and extract Emily. Another team would get the hostages.

Ryan reached the door first, whirling to put his back to the wall on one side. Ice was on the other and their gaz-es met. Fiddler lifted his gun and kicked in the door. Then he tossed in a flashbang and waited.

The noise was deafening. The accompanying flash of light shone as brightly as a lightning strike on a pitch-black night. They entered and began sweeping the area for tangos, taking out four men who tried to regroup and attack them.

Then Ryan bounded for the stairs, taking them two at a time. As he reached the top, he dashed for the room where Emily was being held. Ice and Fiddler were on his heels, and they breached the door in a split second.

But the room was empty. Emily wasn't there. The two men and the other woman weren't there.

"Fuck." Ryan whirled and headed for the stairs again. Outside, gunfire rattled the night. And then the buzzing sound of a helicopter preparing for takeoff cut through the battle noise and speared right into Ryan's ears.

He took off at a run, Fiddler and Iceman with him. They practically jumped from the top of the stairs to the bottom, landing hard but running anyway. Through the building, toward the courtyard, heart pumping, head throbbing, chest ready to explode. There was no one in their way, no movement through the NVGs. He couldn't switch to thermal because he'd lose the real-time targeting for the building.

But it didn't matter because he wasn't going to reach her. They came to the door and kicked it open. The helicopter was already lifting into the air, the rotors whipping the night. Sand swirled in a vortex, grazing their exposed skin, abrading it. He flipped the switch to thermal.

"Don't shoot the chopper," Ryan shouted into his mic in case anyone was planning on bringing it down. "For God's sake, don't shoot. They've got Emily."

TWENTY-SEVEN

THE INSTANT THE POWER HAD gone out, Emily knew what was happening. It was HOT. Her heart thudded and her ears strained for any sound in the night. Raja swore, and then her bodyguard/companion/whatever switched on the light from his phone. Malik did as well.

"This way," Malik said.

The man with Raja gripped Emily's upper arm in hard fingers and rushed her out of the room and down the stairs. She could barely keep up he was so swift, but he kept her on her feet by rushing her along too fast to fall. She'd given him the messenger bag and he'd slung it over his shoulder. She kept thinking about how she could possibly use that as a weapon—grab it and whip it around his neck or something—but he was too quick.

They flew toward the helicopter pad just as the sounds of gunfire erupted in the night. *Come on, HOT. Hurry!*

Emily tried to drag her heels, but it didn't buy much time. The man jerked her forward, his fingers digging into her arm. Raja got into the helicopter just as something exploded in the building they'd left.

A flashbang.

"Ryan," she screamed, and the man slapped a hand over her face. Emily fought for her life, twisting, kicking, biting.

But he was bigger and stronger, and he overpowered her, dragging her toward the chopper before picking her up and tossing her inside. Then he was in the seat in front of her, and Raja was giving the order for the pilot to go even before the door closed or they got strapped in.

Emily looked outside as the helicopter began to lift. She couldn't see anything but the flames from gun barrels as they discharged. A feeling of desperation began to unfurl in her chest, blossoming into a storm of fear and anger.

Raja wanted to take her to Baq, the capital city in Qu'rim. Once there, Emily had no idea what the woman would do to her. And she didn't want to find out.

The helicopter was lifting, hovering—and her microphone crackled.

"Ryan?"

"Emily? Jesus, are you okay? Have they hurt you?"

"Get me out of here," she hissed. "Please get me out of here."

"Honey, we're trying, I swear. But we can't shoot you down. We can't take that chance."

"Raja's on board."

"Doesn't matter, honey. Only you matter."

Emily glanced at the back of her captors' heads. Raja and her bodyguard were preoccupied by the scene below, and Raja urged the pilot in strident language to get them the hell out of there as fast as possible. They'd tossed her into the backseat of the chopper thinking she couldn't get past them, but the door was right there and the slice of it she could reach was big enough to squeeze between the seat in front of her and the body of the craft.

Emily stretched her arm, reaching for the door handle, praying the man wouldn't notice before she had it. And then her fingers closed over it—and the door gave way, swinging wide. The helicopter was gaining altitude, but she only had one choice here.

Only one.

"I'm jumping, Ryan. Catch me."

"Emily, no!"

The man turned as she dove for the opening feet first, cursing and reaching for her, but she slipped out of his grasp, ducking beneath his arm.

They were about twenty feet above the pad now and rising—but if she didn't let go, she'd never make it back home again. A shot rang out and thunked against metal. Ryan swore into his mic—

And Emily let go.

He acted on instinct. He could see her body, see her legs dangling over the edge. And he knew she was going to let go. The helicopter climbed in the sky from twenty feet to twenty-five feet. Soon it would hit thirty and forty.

Ryan threw his rifle aside and sprinted toward the pad, toward Emily, screaming at her not to do it. But he knew she wouldn't listen. He knew she was going to jump. And he had to be there to catch her.

He wasn't quite there yet when her body began to slip, when her legs dangled more and her torso hung out of the helicopter.

"Emily!"

Later, he would say it happened in slow motion, but in fact it happened so fast he couldn't quite say how he managed to get there in time. All he knew was that he put on an extra burst of speed—

And Emily's body dropped from the sky. She was aiming for the sand, he knew that, but if she hit the pad, she'd break every bone in her body. Somehow he was there, beneath her, waiting for her body to make the endless fall into his arms.

She landed against him like a boulder, and they tumbled to the sand together. The air rushed from his body. He couldn't breathe. He wheezed as he tried to drag in air, and his body hurt like a motherfucker.

She was on top of him, the fabric of her abaya limp in his hands as he clutched at her.

"Em," he wheezed. "Em."

She moaned. And then she rolled to the side and cried out. "I think I broke my ankle."

Fiddler and Ice were there suddenly, separating him and Emily. Hands roamed over his limbs, looking for breaks.

The helicopter shot into the sky, rolling toward the horizon. Raja, whoever she was, was gone.

Ryan didn't give a fuck. All he cared about was Emily and making sure she was well.

"I think I broke my ankle," she repeated as Ice examined her.

"Oh sweetie," Ice said gently. "I think you're lucky you didn't break your fucking neck."

Ryan still couldn't speak. It would take a century to get his breath back. He lay there on the ground, faceup, and sucked in air.

"You'll live," Fiddler said after giving him the once-over. "Nothing broken."

"Feel like… hit by truck."

"Yeah, that would be little Emily over here."

"Emily," he forced out, turning his head toward her. He reached out, seeking her hand. She grasped his fingers.

"I'm okay, Ry," she said. "Mostly."

"Stupid. Asinine."

"I know, baby," she told him, patting his hand. "But I wasn't leaving you."

"Yep," Iceman said after a moment. "Broken ankle. Need to splint it."

Ryan wanted to tell Ice and Fiddler to go away, but that was impossible right now. They were still in the middle of a mission, and they had to make it onto the Blackhawks that would be here at any moment.

Around them, the sounds of battle subsided as HOT mopped up what was left of the Freedom Force cell.

"Well, that's considerate of them," Big Mac said as he strode up with his gun slung in front of his body and greasepaint on his face. "A helicopter pad's going to make this much easier."

Ryan could hear the Blackhawks coming. His body still hurt, but his breath was coming back. He pushed himself to a sitting position, Emily's hand clasped in his. She was sitting up too now. She had her head turned as Ice worked to splint her ankle. And then her fingers squeezed his and she gasped.

"Sorry," Ice said. "I'll give you something for the pain when we're on the Blackhawk."

"It's okay," she said. "It could be worse."

Yeah, she could have broken her back. Split her head open. Ryan shuddered to think of what could have happened to her. He wanted to haul her close and not let go, but he still had a job to do. He kissed her fingers and pushed to his feet as the hostages emerged from the building, escorted by Knight Rider, Brandy, Double Dee, and a couple of the Echo Squad guys.

"Oh, they *were* here," Emily said. "Thank God."

"Gotta go help with them," he said roughly, trying to stem the emotion in his voice.

She looked up at him, her eyes shining. "I know you do… Find me later, okay?"

He bent and kissed her swiftly on the mouth. "I'll always find you, Emily," he said against her lips.

Then he turned and walked away.

Emily thought she would see Ryan when they were extracted, but it didn't happen that way. Three Blackhawk helicopters arrived, and she was put onto the first one that landed, along with the sick and injured hostages. She protested that she wasn't sick, but it didn't matter. Ice put her on the helicopter, climbed in beside her, and fished in his pack for a needle and a vial.

"Now don't you think of jumping out of this thing," he told her right before he stuck her.

"I won't," she grumbled, wincing. "That was a special circumstance."

He snorted. "Yeah, special." Then he grinned and chucked her on the shoulder. "You're crazy, Em, but you're all right. Good work today."

She ducked her head, embarrassed and angry with herself. "I got captured, and then I let Raja get away with the money."

Ice blinked. He was rough around the edges and gorgeous as sin, but he didn't make her heart skip beats the way Ryan did.

"Hey, you led us to them. We defeated a cell and got everyone out alive. I'd say that's a good fucking day. Don't worry about the rest—besides, you saw her face. That's got to count for something."

It was Emily's turn to blink. She'd been so focused on what she hadn't done that she didn't think about what she had. "Wow. I did, didn't I?"

That was good for some drawings at least. And maybe someone would recognize Raja based on her description. She wasn't likely to forget the woman anytime soon. She'd been stunning, and cruel. A beauty whose inside didn't match the outside.

"Yeah, so keep thinking about the details. They're valuable."

He moved on to treat other passengers, and she leaned her head back against the side of the helicopter and tried to focus on those last few minutes when she'd known she had to jump or she'd never see Ryan again.

"Excuse me," a woman said, and Emily turned to look at her. "Are we safe? Are we really safe now?"

Her voice quivered, and Emily reached over, put her hand on the woman's arm. "Yes, we're safe now. You're with the best of the best—you're going home."

The woman sucked in her breath on a sob. "Oh thank God." Tears streaked down her dirty cheeks. "My baby—I don't know if my baby is okay. I don't know."

Emily's heart squeezed. She wrapped her arm around Linda Cooper and hugged her close. "You'll be fine, Linda. You really will."

She didn't know for certain, but she prayed it was so.

Linda trembled from head to toe. "You know my name."

"Yes, you're Linda Cooper. Your husband is Major Cooper—and you're going home to him at Aviano Air Base. You're going home."

Linda stared at her for a long moment—and then she collapsed against Emily's shoulder and cried. Emily held her, patting her from time to time, her own eyes filling with tears.

Linda Cooper was safe and she was going home to her husband. But what was Emily going home to? She had no idea. Ryan had saved her when she'd jumped, and he'd kissed her before he'd left. But what did he *feel?*

She still didn't know. And did it even matter? He cared, she knew that much was true, and he wanted to marry her. She closed her eyes and laid her cheek on Linda's hair. *He wanted to marry her*. It would have to be enough.

TWENTY-EIGHT

EMILY AND THE HOSTAGES WERE taken to Land-stuhl Regional Medical Center in Germany. When they'd reached the air base and the transport waiting to fly them out of the Middle East, Emily argued that she didn't need to go. What she really wanted was to be with HOT, to fly where they flew, and to see Ryan.

But he wasn't there. She didn't know where he was as she got loaded onto the medevac flight. Then the doors closed and they were on their way. In Germany, she was thoroughly checked out. Her ankle was broken, she was almost twelve weeks pregnant—she didn't understand pregnancy dating, but whatever—and the baby had a strong heartbeat. Relief flooded her as she heard it beat for the first time.

And then she promptly burst into tears. There was a miraculous little thing inside her, and it was alive and well. But Ryan wasn't there to share the moment with her, and that made her cry harder. The technician simply handed her tissues and waited. Apparently women bursting into tears the first time they heard their baby's heartbeat wasn't all that unusual.

They kept her overnight for observation. Standard procedure, she was told. She was put into a room with Linda Cooper, which was nice, and they chatted from time to time. And then sometime during the middle of the night, she was awakened as a man came into the room.

Her heart thumped hard, but he wasn't there for her. It was Major Cooper, and he went to his wife's side and broke down. Emily tried not to cry, but it was impossible. She turned her head into her pillow and let the tears soak the fabric as Linda and her husband cried and laughed and hugged.

A nurse came in and told Major Cooper he had to leave and let his wife rest, but he begged to stay with her. The nurse finally relented, and he spent the night in a recliner beside her bed. Emily fell asleep eventually. When she woke again, she turned and saw Major Cooper's boots in the recliner. She couldn't see him or Linda because the nurse had pulled the curtain, but she smiled as a snore came from the other side of the barrier.

Then she turned the other way—and her heart leapt into her throat. There was a man in a chair. He was slumped over, arms crossed, his forehead on his arms. No comfy recliner for her Special Ops warrior.

"Ryan?"

His body stiffened—and then his head snapped up, his eyes red-rimmed with lack of sleep. He'd tried to wash off the greasepaint, but there were still traces of it here and there. He had a day's growth of beard, his hair was shaggy, and his blue eyes bored into her.

She'd never seen a more handsome man in her life.

He was on his feet and by her side in an instant. "I'm

here, Emily. I said I'd be here."

His voice was scratchy and he smelled like the desert. If sand trickled from his clothes onto the floor, she wouldn't be surprised.

He took her hand and kissed it. She lifted her other hand and ran it over that rough jaw. "You said you'd find me. You did."

"That's right."

"I thought I wouldn't see you until we were back in DC. I thought it would be days—maybe weeks."

"No fucking way," he growled.

"I didn't want to go without you," she whispered. "They wouldn't let me stay and wait for you."

He threaded his fingers through her hair. "No, we had to get you to safety. But here you are, and here I am. It worked out."

"How are you?" Because she knew she'd hit hard when she'd landed on him.

He grinned. "Feel like I got hit by a truck, but otherwise I'm okay."

"I'm so sorry. I panicked—if I hadn't jumped... She would have killed me, Ry. She wanted information on HOT, and she would have killed me after she'd tortured it out of me."

"I know, honey. I know you had to do it—but Jesus, you scared the shit out of me. It could have ended up so much worse, Emily."

"But it didn't. I'm here."

He let his gaze slide down her body. "Yeah, with a broken ankle and probably a few bruises too."

"But the baby's fine."

"I know, and I'm sorry I couldn't be here with you. I

know you must have been scared."

She squeezed his hand. "I was. But you're here now, and everything's going to be okay."

But then she remembered something Raja had said, and a current of fear snapped through her.

"What is it, honey?"

"Raja... she said they knew who I was and who I cared for. And she said we would pay."

Ryan squeezed her hand. "You're under HOT's protection, Emily. The only one who's going to pay is Raja and her Freedom Force. We'll get them."

She bit her lip. "What if she sends someone after me in DC? What then? We don't really know what she's capable of."

His expression was fierce. "She'll have to go through me—and that won't be easy, I promise. Besides, she has far bigger things to worry about than a woman who got away."

Emily sucked in a breath and let it out again slowly. "You're right." Because she knew what sort of people the Freedom Force attracted, and she knew they thrived on fomenting terror. In the scheme of things, she wasn't important to them. If it was convenient to punish her, they would. But they wouldn't waste resources to go after her when they had far more important battles—to them—to fight.

"You remember what she looks like?"

"Yes."

"Good. When we get home, you can tell Mendez everything. He'll do everything he can to find her."

She frowned as she studied their linked hands. "I'm not sure my name will be cleared. I may still be the same

Emily bin Yusuf I have been—on watch lists and no-fly lists, and with no hope of ever getting off those lists again. If you spend time with me, you'll be tainted by association. Your career will be over."

He put his fingers beneath her chin and forced her to look at him. What she saw in his eyes made her breath catch.

"Listen good, Emily, because I mean for you to understand this the first time I say it. I don't give a good goddamn about anything but you and our baby. I love you, and if I have to be a civilian who never leaves the United States, then so be it. No one's going to stop me from getting a job or taking care of our family. You're all I need. All I want. If I have to plow fields to be with you, then I'd better go get some shit-kickers and a cowboy hat and figure out how to operate a tractor. Because if that's what it takes, that's what I'm doing. You got that?"

She tried not to burst into tears, but damn if the hormones raging through her body didn't make that impossible. With every word he spoke, her eyes filled until the tears spilled over and ran down her cheeks. When he finished, she launched herself at him and threw her arms around his neck. He bent over the bed, his arms going around her, pulling her as close as he could.

And then he kissed her, his mouth crushing down on hers, his tongue sliding inside to glide against hers in a delicious back-and-forth that made her breasts tingle and her pussy ache. If they were alone—oh God, if they were alone! The things she'd do to him. The things she'd ask for. It was dirty and hot and oh so thrilling to imagine.

She wanted more than to imagine, but that wasn't going to happen in this room. He broke the kiss sooner than she would have liked and lowered her down to the bed.

"We have to stop," he muttered. "I can't take this."

She laughed softly, her vision still blurry from happy tears. "Me neither. Oh Ryan, do you really love me? Is that possible after everything?"

He blinked. "You're fucking kidding, right? Of course I love you. I've loved you since the first moment I saw you." He held up a hand when she would have protested, and she bit her tongue to keep from speaking and ruining the moment. "It's true. I'd never seen anything more beautiful in my life or anyone I wanted more."

"You're crazy," she whispered.

"Crazy for you. And it's okay if you don't feel the same way. I know you've been through a lot, and it takes time—"

She put her hand over his mouth. He really didn't know? How was that possible? She'd been nothing but starry-eyed around him for months. And then there was the night she'd begged him to make love to her...

"For someone whose life pretty much relies on knowing what's happening around him, your lack of observational skills worries me. Don't you know, Ryan Gordon, that I've been in love with you for months? Maybe not from the first moment, but close. I think when I saw you at Jack and Gina's place, right after Nick and Victoria got engaged, that's the moment I knew I'd fallen for you. So yes, you gorgeous idiot, I love you. I've loved you for a long, long time."

She drew her hand away from his mouth then. His mouth was open a little, his eyes wide. And then he swooped down and kissed her again, hard and long and deep, and she wrapped her arms around him as happiness burst inside her soul. Real happiness—and belonging. They belonged to each other, and she would be forever grateful for that fact.

TWENTY-NINE

Two weeks later…

IT WAS THE FASTEST-PLANNED WEDDING in the history of weddings. Ryan had suggested they get married right away and then have a big wedding after the baby was born, like Matt and Evie planned on doing, but Emily said she didn't care about that. All she cared about was having her friends and family together on their special day.

And so they were married at Jack and Gina's sprawling Eastern Shore estate, with a string quartet and catering by a local firm that did weddings and parties. Ryan was suspicious of the whole thing since the costs weren't all that much, but he wasn't about to demand that Gina Domenico, international superstar, tell him if she'd footed the lion's share of the bill as he suspected.

The gardens had been turned into a fairy-tale setting with a big white tent, tables draped in white cloths and set with silver, crystal, and china. There was an arbor with white roses tucked away over the entire length of it, and the preacher stood serenely with his Bible. Ryan wore his

Army dress uniform and stood beside the preacher, nervous and wondering if Emily might change her mind before she walked—or hobbled, more likely—down the aisle.

His father was his best man. Dave Gordon hadn't expressed surprise so much as a quiet satisfaction when Ryan called him and announced he was getting married. Ryan had been a little worried about what his father would think, but he'd been nothing but happy. And he'd gotten on a plane and come from his home in Colorado on short notice so he could be there.

Victoria was Emily's maid of honor and she stood across the aisle, looking serene even though Ryan knew she was anything but. Boy did he know.

The audience was filled with members of Alpha and Echo squads, as well as some of the HOT support staff. Gina Domenico Hunter sat with her husband and young son and looked entirely too pleased with herself as she rocked her newborn in her arms.

Yeah, she'd orchestrated this whole thing… and Ryan wanted to give her a big hug for it. He didn't much care about a fancy wedding, but didn't all little girls dream of one? Emily had said she didn't care, but what if she did? Gina had fixed it so they'd never find out if Emily would regret not having the fairy-tale day.

The string quartet struck up the wedding march and everyone stood. Emily appeared at the end of the aisle on Colonel Mendez's arm. Ryan had been surprised when Emily said she wanted the colonel to give her away. But Emily, with her usual way of cutting through things, said that Mendez was responsible for all the good that had happened in her and Victoria's lives recently. He'd given Victoria a job, and he'd done his best to give Emily a normal life after she'd returned from Qu'rim the first time. Not only that, but he was also the HOT commander—and without HOT, neither Emily nor Victoria would have their happily-ever-afters.

The colonel was sharp in his dress uniform with the eagles on his shoulders, but Emily outshone them all.

She wore a simple white dress that floated around her like she was a princess. It was strapless satin with a wide belt at the waist, and it flowed in one long silken wave to the ground. When she moved, it rippled around her. The only embellishment the dress needed was Emily.

Her golden hair was piled elaborately on her head, and a long veil was clipped somewhere in those curls and floated behind her. She had on a pearl necklace and earrings, and she carried a white bouquet.

Her smile was huge as she hobbled slowly down the aisle on the colonel's arm, and Ryan thought he might drop to his knees they went so weak. Somehow he managed to stay standing.

His father gently elbowed him. "You gonna make it, son?" he whispered.

"Yes, sir. Definitely. You still got the ring?"

"Yes."

The colonel stopped and the preacher asked who was giving this woman in matrimony.

"I am," Colonel Mendez said, and then he stepped up and put Emily's hand into Ryan's.

When their fingers touched, a shiver of anticipation went through him. Her brown eyes didn't leave his as he tucked her arm into the crook of his own.

The preacher began the ceremony, but all Ryan could think about was that this woman belonged to him. This remarkable, amazing woman who'd suffered through so much but who still had a resounding and optimistic spirit.

When it was time for the vows, Ryan knew what he planned to say. He and Emily faced each other, holding hands, and he looked into her eyes, seeing only love and acceptance there. He cleared his throat, knowing he was about to say words that might not be the most eloquent, but were the most heartfelt.

"Emily, you've taught me something about myself these past few months since I've known you. You're the bravest, best person I know, and you've taught me that no one has to let their wounds define them. You've taught me that happiness isn't predefined. Happiness is what you make it, what you let it make you. Happiness is as simple as a woman's smile—*your* smile—and as complex as our baby growing inside you. I'm honored and bewildered that you've chosen me, but I vow to you that I will love you with everything I am and everything I ever will be. I will stand beside you, and I will stand between you and the world when you need me to. I will guard your heart, your feelings, and I will never let anyone harm you. I will be your rock in a storm and your anchor when you need it. You are everything to me, and I intend to make sure you know it for the rest of our lives."

There were tears in her eyes as she squeezed his hands. Then she dropped her gaze and cleared her throat. When she looked up again, her eyes were still shining, but she seemed to have it under control.

"Ryan, when you look at me, you don't see someone whose mistakes define her. You never have. I have always felt like you've seen me, the real me, and I've been amazed that you didn't judge me for the things I've done.

But that's because you're the kindest, most amazing man I've ever known. You see the good in people, and you made me believe that I was better than I thought I was. You made me see the good in me again. I can never thank you enough for that. I love you so much it scares me, and I'm still stunned you love me. I'm the luckiest woman alive and I know it. I promise to love you forever, and I promise to take care of you and honor you. I'll be beside you no matter what, and yes, I will defend you when I have to. I know you don't think that'll happen since you're way bigger than I am—"

Here people laughed, and he was glad because his heart was hammering and he was beginning to seriously doubt his ability to keep from shedding a tear as she talked.

"—But just in case it does, I want you to know I'm here. I vow to be the best partner, the best mother, and I vow to always let you be the first to know if I get any offers to join another mercenary group—"

More laughter. Hell, even he laughed.

"—Mostly I just vow to love you for who you are. You make me better, Ryan, and I need you."

The preacher was still pronouncing them man and wife when Ryan dragged her into his arms and kissed her. It was a real kiss, not a sweet kiss for pictures or a kiss to prevent her lipstick from smearing.

No, he intended to smear her lipstick. And then he intended to carry her to his car and drive her to their hotel just as soon as he could decently do so, because he intended to mess up a lot more than her lipstick.

Vaguely, he realized people were cheering. Somehow he set Emily away from him. She laughed and pulled a tissue from somewhere, then she was wiping lipstick from his mouth. They walked down the aisle as the quartet played, through an honor guard of swords, and into the tent where the reception was being held.

Before he could say anything to her, they were set upon by well-wishers. Their friends laughed and offered congratulations. The men shook hands and the women kissed. His heart was full as he looked out over the gathering. His father was smiling and talking to the colonel, which made Ryan wonder how on earth anyone ever relaxed enough to smile at Colonel Mendez. The man exuded a raw energy that had you wondering what he was up to at all times.

Victoria appeared in front of him then, and he almost took a step back. He'd barely talked to her since they'd returned from the desert, but he knew she hadn't been pleased with him. Even marrying Emily hadn't been enough for her. She'd spent the past week at HOT HQ glaring at him—and when he'd walked onto the pistol range and she'd been standing there, grinning at him as she picked up her gun and shot the fucking target dead center without looking at it, he'd begun to seriously wonder if he'd survive the next mission they went on together.

But now she stood in front of him with tears in her eyes. Then she wrapped her arms around him and hugged him, and he almost wondered if he should be wary of a knife.

She stepped back and swiped beneath her eyes, and he nearly breathed a sigh of relief.

"I wasn't sure about any of this, I'll admit it," she said. "But those vows—my God, you love her. You really do."

"Yeah, I do."

Her smile was wide and pretty. "Then that's enough for me. Congratulations, Flash. And thanks for everything."

"No, thank you. You've always believed in her and never stopped looking for her. I didn't know her then, but I'm glad you didn't give up. If you had…"

He shuddered to think that he might not have ever met Emily. That she might not have gotten free before it was too late.

Victoria squeezed his hand and then left him to go over and slip into Brandy's arms.

Soon Ryan and Emily sat and listened to speeches while everyone was served dinner. After dinner, there was dancing. They danced their first dance together as man and wife with everyone cheering and clapping. After that, the party took off.

Knight Rider and Georgie Hayes were wrapped in each other's arms on the dance floor. Matt and Evie sat with heads together and private smiles on their faces. Evie fed a piece of cake to Matt with her fingers, and the look he gave her was so intense that Ryan quickly looked away.

Ice and Grace were holding hands and laughing at something Billy the Kid was saying while his wife Olivia shook her head and pretended to be exasperated with him. Hawk was holding the baby while Gina chased after little Eli and the frog he'd picked up from the grass.

Everyone else was dancing, talking, laughing, eating, and having a good time. Ryan sat up a little straighter as he realized what that meant.

"They're not paying attention to us anymore. Think we've been here long enough?" he asked in an aside to

Emily.

"God, I hope so."

He took her hand and stood. No one seemed to care as they snuck out of the tent.

A shape loomed ahead of them. Ryan had started to shove Emily behind him when that shape passed under a light and became Colonel Mendez. Ryan didn't want to think about the verbal lashing he'd endured from the colonel once his involvement with Emily became known, but it was kind of hard not to remember the exact moment a full-bird called you on the carpet and threatened to remove your balls through your throat.

Thankfully, he'd survived the encounter. And the colonel had agreed to give Emily away as soon as she asked him, which had to be a good sign. Still, Ryan was slightly bitter that he'd had his ass reamed while Emily got the sweet teddy bear colonel. Why couldn't he have gotten the sweet teddy bear colonel?

Uh, on second thought…

"Sir," Ryan said, snapping a salute since they were in uniform and outdoors.

The colonel returned the salute. "Sergeant. Emily." He reached into his pocket and pulled out an envelope that he held out to Emily. "Ian Black wanted you to have this."

She took it and looked up at Ryan. "Open it," he told her because he wanted to get whatever it was out of the way. He didn't think Black was going to ruin their wedding or anything, but he wanted to know what it was so they could get on with the rest of their lives.

She stuck her thumbnail under the flap and lifted. Then she pulled out a piece of cream paper and unfolded it. Her hand slapped over her mouth.

"He did it," she said after a long moment. "He kept his promise. Emily bin Yusuf never existed. There's Emily Royal and Emily Gordon. No one else—and no more restrictions."

"That's right," Mendez said. "I don't know how he managed it, but Ian has... methods... that aren't necessarily available to the rest of us."

That was a polite way of saying Ian Black was a rogue and a son of a bitch who operated outside the strictures of the law. But damn, he'd just delivered on his promise to Emily, and that was enough to make Ryan feel a few warm fuzzies toward him. Temporarily, anyway.

Emily's eyes were wide as she turned to him. "Ryan, we can go to the Caribbean if we want. Or Europe. We can go anywhere!" She whirled to the colonel. "He won't have to leave HOT now, right? It's okay if he stays?"

Colonel Mendez smiled for at least the second time that day. Ian Black keeping a promise and now this? What was the world coming to?

"Emily, he wasn't ever leaving. I wouldn't let that happen... And speaking of HOT, think you might want to help us out a bit?"

"I... doing what?"

"You know things about the Freedom Force, and you've seen Raja. Already the sketches from your description are helping us narrow down who she might be. You can keep helping us—with intel, with advice on language and tactics. Use your expertise."

Ryan could tell that she was stunned by this offer. Hell, so was he. But it wasn't fieldwork. He reminded himself of that. Mendez wasn't sending a pregnant woman into the field no matter what.

"I'd like that," she said. And then she squeezed Ryan's hand. "But only if my husband doesn't have a problem with my doing it."

Her answer shocked him. And humbled him. He'd given her such a hard time in Acamar. He'd been scared senseless for her, and he was happier than hell she was out of there—but she'd accomplished things no one else could have done. How could he tell her she couldn't help when she'd been so worried about *his* career with HOT and how it would affect him to give it up?

"Emily, I want you to do whatever makes you happy. If you want to work for HOT, I think you'd be a great asset."

Her smile was like sunshine to him. "Thank you for saying that." She turned to Mendez. "I'd be happy to consult, Colonel. I want to help my country in any way I can."

"Excellent. We'll see you at HQ soon then."

"Yes, soon."

The colonel left them, and they hurried to the front of the house and found Ryan's car, giggling like children sneaking around. Soon they were at the hotel, and Ryan came around to get her out of the car. He carried her to the front desk and then up the stairs and over the threshold.

When he had her naked, when he'd worshiped every inch of her body with his hands and mouth and made her come half a dozen times, he positioned himself over top of her and thrust into her willing body with one smooth move.

And then he stilled, his heart pounding and his throat aching with emotion. This was home. Being inside Emily and feeling her lovely body wrapping around his. Knowing she was his forever. Knowing life with her would only get better and better.

"What's wrong?" she asked when he didn't move.

He had to swallow the knot in his throat. "Wrong? Nothing's wrong, honey. Everything's right."

She smiled up at him and cupped his cheeks in her palms. "It is, isn't it?"

"Yeah, it is."

It had begun in the desert sands of Qu'rim the night he'd met her. It wouldn't end until the moment he died.

ABOUT THE AUTHOR

LYNN RAYE HARRIS is the *New York Times* and *USA Today* bestselling author of the HOSTILE OPERATIONS TEAM SERIES of military romances as well as 20 books for Harlequin Presents. A former finalist for the Romance Writers of America's Golden Heart Award and the National Readers Choice Award, Lynn lives in Alabama with her handsome former military husband and two crazy cats. Lynn's books have been called "exceptional and emotional," "intense," and "sizzling." Lynn's books have sold over 2 million copies worldwide.

Connect with me online:
Facebook: https://www.facebook.com/AuthorLynnRayeHarris
Twitter: https://twitter.com/LynnRayeHarris
Website: http://www.LynnRayeHarris.com
Email: lynn@lynnrayeharris.com

Join my Hostile Operations Team Readers and Fans Group on Facebook:
https://www.facebook.com/groups/HOTReadersAndFans/

CPSIA information can be obtained
at www.ICGtesting.com
Printed in the USA
FFOW03n2345291215
20053FF

9 781941 002070